A MONTH TO MARRY THE MIDWIFE

BY
FIONA McARTHUR

Published in Great Britain 2017
By Mills & Boon, an imprint of HarperCollins*Publishers*
1 London Bridge Street, London, SE1 9GF

© 2017 Fiona McArthur

ISBN: 978-0-263-92637-8

Printed and bound in Spain
by CPI, Barcelona

Fiona McArthur is an Australian midwife who lives in the country and loves to dream. Writing Medical Romance gives Fiona the scope to write about all the wonderful aspects of romance, adventure, medicine and the midwifery she feels so passionate about. When she's not catching babies, Fiona and her husband, Ian, are off to meet new people, see new places and have wonderful adventures. Drop in and say hi at Fiona's website: FionaMcArthurAuthor.com.

Books by Fiona McArthur

Mills & Boon Medical Romance

Christmas in Lyrebird Lake

Midwife's Christmas Proposal
Midwife's Mistletoe Baby

A Doctor, A Fling & A Wedding Ring
The Prince Who Charmed Her
Gold Coast Angels: Two Tiny Heartbeats
Christmas with Her Ex

Visit the Author Profile page
at millsandboon.co.uk for more titles.

Dedicated to Rosie, who sprinted with me on this one,
Trish, who walked the beach with me, and Flo,
who rode the new wave and kept me afloat.
What a fab journey with awesome friends.

PROLOGUE

THE WHITE SAND curved away in a crescent as Ellie Swift descended to Lighthouse Bay Beach and turned towards the bluff. When she stepped onto the beach the luscious crush of cool, fine sand under her toes made her suck in her breath with a grin and the ocean breeze tasted salty against her lips. Ellie set off at a brisk pace towards the edge of the waves to walk the bay to the headland and back before she needed to dress for work.

'Ellie!'

She spun, startled, away from the creamy waves now washing her feet, and saw a man limping towards her. He waved again. Jeff, from the surf club. Ellie knew Jeff, the local prawn-trawler captain and chief lifesaver. She'd delivered his second son. Jeff had fainted and Ellie tried not to remind him of that every time she saw him.

She waved back but already suspected the call wasn't social. She turned and sped up to meet him.

'We've got an old guy down on the rocks under the lighthouse, a surfer, says he's your doctor from the hospital. We think he's busted his arm, and maybe a leg.'

Ellie turned her head to look towards the headland Jeff had come from.

Jeff waved his hand towards the huddle of people in the distance. 'He won't let anybody touch him until you come. The ambulance is on the way but I reckon we might have to chopper him out from here.'

Ellie worked all over the hospital so it wasn't unusual that she was who people asked for. An old guy and a surfer. That was Dr Southwell. She sighed.

Ten minutes later Ellie was kneeling beside the good doctor, guarding his wrinkled neck in a brace as she watched the two ambulance women and two burly life-savers carefully shift him onto the rescue frame. Then it was done. Just a small groan escaped his gritted teeth as he closed his eyes and let the pain from the move-ment slowly subside.

Ellie glanced at the ocean, lying aqua and innocent, as if to say, *it wasn't my fault*, and suspected Dr South-well would doggedly heal and return to surfing with renewed vigour as soon as he could. The tide was on the way out and the waves weren't reaching the sloping plateau at the base of the cliffs any more where the life-savers had secured their casualty. The spot was popular with intrepid surfers to climb on and off their boards and paddle into the warm swell and out to the waves.

'Thanks for coming, Ellie.' Dr Southwell was look-ing much more comfortable and a trifle sheepish. 'Sorry to leave you in the lurch on the ward.'

She smiled at him. He'd always been sweet. 'Don't

you worry about us. Look after you. They'll get you sorted once you've landed. Get well soon.'

The older man closed his eyes briefly. Then he winked at Ellie. 'I'll be back. As soon as I can.'

Ellie smiled and shook her head. He'd gone surfing every morning before his clinic, the athletic spring to his step contradicting his white hair and weathered face, a tall, thin gentleman who must have been a real catch fifty years ago. They'd splinted his arm against his body, didn't think the leg was broken, but they were treating it as such and had administered morphine, having cleared it with the helicopter flight nurse on route via mobile phone.

In the distance the *thwump-thwump* of the helicopter rotor could be heard approaching. Ellie knew how efficient the rescue team was. He'd be on his way very shortly.

Ellie glanced at the sweeping bay on the other side from where they crouched—the white sand that curved like a new moon around the bay, the rushing of the tide through the fish-filled creek back into the sea—and could understand why he'd want to return.

This place had stopped her wandering too. She lifted her chin. Lighthouse Bay held her future and she had plans for the hospital.

She looked down at the man, a gentle man in the true sense of the word, who had fitted so beautifully into the calm pace of the bay. 'We'll look forward to you coming back. As soon as you're well.' She glanced at the enormous Malibu surfboard the lifesavers had propped up against the cliff face. 'I'll get one of the guys to drop your board at my house and it will be there waiting for you.'

Ellie tried very hard not to think about the next few days. *Damn.* Now they didn't have an on-call doctor and the labouring women would have to be transferred to the base hospital until another locum arrived. She needed to move quickly on those plans to make her maternity ward a midwifery group practice.

CHAPTER ONE

FOUR DAYS LATER, outside Ellie's office at the maternity ward at Lighthouse Bay Hospital, a frog croaked. It was very close outside her window. She shuddered as she assembled the emergency locum-doctor's welcome pack. Head down, she concentrated on continuing the task and pretended not to see the tremor in her fingers as she gathered the papers. She was a professional in charge of a hospital, for goodness' sake. Her ears strained for a repeat of the dreaded noise and hoped like heck she wouldn't hear it. She strained...but thankfully silence ensued.

'Concentrate on the task,' she muttered. She included a local map, which after the first day they wouldn't need because the town was so small, but it covered everywhere they could eat.

A list of the hours they were required to man the tiny doctor's clinic—just two in total on the other side of the hospital on each day of the week they were here. Then, in a month, hand over to the other local doctor who had threatened to leave if he didn't get holidays.

She couldn't blame him or his wife—they deserved a

life! It was getting busier. Dr Rodgers, an elderly bachelor, had done the call-outs before he'd become ill. She hummed loudly to drown out the sound of the little voice that suggested she should have a life too, and of course to drown out the frogs. Ellie concentrated as she printed out the remuneration package.

The idea that any low-risk woman who went into labour would have to be transferred to the large hospital an hour away from her family just because no locum doctor could come was wrong. Especially when she'd had all her antenatal care with Ellie over the last few months. So the locum doctors were a necessary evil. It wasn't an onerous workload for them, in fact, because the midwives did all the maternity work, and the main hospital was run as a triage station with a nurse practitioner, as they did in the Outback, so actually the locums only covered the hospital for emergencies and recovering inpatient needs.

Ellie dreamed of the day their maternity unit was fully self-sufficient. She quite happily played with the idea that she could devote her whole life to the project, get a nurse manager and finally step away from general nursing.

She could employ more midwives like her friend and neighbour Trina, who lived in one of the cliff houses. The young widowed midwife from the perfect marriage who preferred night duty so she didn't lie awake at night alone in her bed.

She was the complete opposite to Ellie, who'd had the marriage from hell that hadn't turned out to be a marriage at all.

Then there was Faith who did the evening shifts, the young mum who lived with her aunt and her three-year-old son. Faith was their eternal optimist. She hadn't found a man to practise heartbreak on yet. Just had an unfortunate one-night stand with a charismatic drifter. Ellie sighed. Three diverse women with a mutual dream. Lighthouse Bay Mothers and Babies. A gentle place for families to discover birth with midwives.

Back to the real world. For the moment they needed the championship of at least one GP/OB.

Most new mums stayed between one and three nights and, as they always had, women post-caesarean birth transferred back from the base hospital to recover. So a ward round in maternity and the general part of the hospital each morning by the VMO was asked to keep the doors open.

The tense set of her shoulders gradually relaxed as she distracted herself with the chore she'd previously completed six times since old Dr Rodgers had had his stroke.

The first two locums had been young and bored, patently here for the surf, and had both tried to make advances towards Ellie, as if she were part of the locum package. She'd had no problem freezing them both back into line but now the agency took on board her preferences for mature medical practitioners.

Most replacements had been well into retirement age since then, though there had also been some disadvantages with their advanced age. The semi-bald doctor definitely had been grumpy, which had been a bit of a disappointment, because Dr Rodgers had always had a kind word for everyone.

The next had been terrified that a woman would give birth and he'd have to do something about it because he hadn't been near a baby's delivery for twenty years. Ellie hadn't been able to promise one wouldn't happen so he'd declined to come back.

Lighthouse Bay was a service for low-risk pregnant women so Ellie couldn't see what the concern was. Birth was a perfectly normal, natural event and the women weren't sick. But there would always be those occasional precipitous and out-of-the-ordinary labours that seemed to happen more since Ellie had arrived. She'd proven well equal to the task of catching impatient babies but a decent back-up made sense. So, obstetric confidence was a second factor she requested now from the locums.

The next three locums had been either difficult to contact when she'd needed them or had driven her mad by sitting and talking all day so she hadn't been able to get anything done, so she hadn't asked them back. But the last locum had finally proved a golden one.

Dr Southwell, the elderly widower and retired GP with his obstetric diploma and years of gentle experience, had been a real card.

The postnatal women had loved him, as had every other marriageable woman above forty in town.

Especially Myra, Ellie's other neighbour, a retired chef who donated two hours a day to the hospital café between morning tea and lunch, and used to run a patisserie in Double Bay in Sydney. Myra and Old Dr Southwell had often been found laughing together.

Ellie had thought the hospital had struck the jackpot when he'd enquired about a more permanent position and had stayed full-time for an extra month when the last local GP had asked for an extended holiday. Ellie had really appreciated the break from trying to understand each new doctor's little pet hates.

Not that Dr Southwell seemed to have any foible Ellie had had to grow accustomed to at all. Except his love of surfing. She sighed.

They'd already sent one woman away in the last two days because she'd come to the hospital having gone into early labour. Ellie had had to say they had no locum coverage and she should drive to the base hospital.

Croak... There it was again. A long-drawn-out, guttural echo promising buckets of slime... She sucked in air through her nose and forced herself to breathe the constricted air out. She had to fight the resistance because her lungs seemed to have shrunk back onto her ribcage.

Croak... And then the *cruk-cruk* of the mate. She glanced at the clock and estimated she had an hour at least before the new doctor arrived so she reached over, turned on the CD player and allowed her favourite country singer to protect her from the noise as he belted out a southern ballad that drowned out the neighbours. Thankfully, today, her only maternity patient had brought her the latest CD from the large town an hour away where she'd gone for her repeat Caesarean birth.

It was only rarely, after prolonged rain, that the frogs

gave her such a hard time. They'd had a week of down-pours. Of course frogs were about. They'd stop soon. The rain had probably washed away the solution of salt water she'd sprayed around the outside of the ward window, so she'd do it again this afternoon.

One of the bonuses of her tiny croft cottage on top of the cliff was that, up there, the salt-laden spray from waves crashing against the rocks below drove the amphibians away.

She knew it was ridiculous to have a phobia about frogs, but she had suffered with it since she was little. It was inextricably connected to the time not long after her mother had died. She knew perfectly well it was irrational.

She had listened to the tapes, seen the psychologist, had even been transported by hypnosis to the causative events in an attempt to reprogram her response. That had actually made it worse, because now she had the childhood nightmares back that hadn't plagued her for years.

Basically slimy, web-footed frogs with fat throats that ballooned hideously when they croaked made her palms sweat and her heart beat like a drum in her chest. And the nightmares made her weep with grief in her sleep.

Unfortunately, down in the hollow where the old hospital nestled among well-grown shrubs and an enticing tinge of dampness after rain, the frogs were very happy to congregate. Her only snake in Eden. Actually, she could do with a big, quiet carpet snake that enjoyed green entrées. That could be the answer. She had no phobia of snakes.

But those frogs that slipped insidiously into the hand basin in the ladies' rest room—no way! Or those that croaked outside the door so that when she arrived as she had this morning, running a little late, a little incautiously intent on getting to work, a green tree frog had jumped at her as she'd stepped through the door. Thank goodness he'd missed his aim.

She still hadn't recovered from that traumatic start to her day. Now they were outside her window... Her hero sang on and she determined to stop thinking about it. She did not have time for this.

Samuel Southwell parked his now dusty Lexus outside the cottage hospital. His immaculate silver machine had never been off the bitumen before, and he frowned at the rim of dust that clung to the base of the windscreen.

He noted with a feeling of unreality, the single *Reserved for Doctor* spot in the car park, and his hand hovered as he hesitated to stop the engine. *Doctor.* Not plural. Just one spot for the one doctor. He couldn't remember the last time he'd been without a cloud of registrars, residents and med students trailing behind him.

What if they wanted him to look at a toenail or someone had a heart attack? He was a consultant obstetrician and medical researcher, for heaven's sake.

At that thought his mouth finally quirked. Surely his knowledge of general medicine was buried miraculously in his brain underneath the uteruses? He sincerely hoped so or he'd have to refresh his knowledge of whatever ailment stumped him. Online medical journals could be accessed. According to his father it shouldn't be a problem—he was 'supposed to be smart'!

Maybe the old man was right and it would do him good. Either way, he'd agreed, mainly because his dad never asked him to do anything and he'd been strangely persistent about this favour. This little place had less than sixty low-risk births a year. And he was only here for the next four weeks. He would manage.

It would be vastly different from the peaks of drama skimmed from thousands of women and babies passing through the doors of Brisbane Mothers and Babies Hospital. Different being away from his research work that drove him at nights and weekends. He'd probably get more sleep as well. He admired his father but at the moment he was a little impatient with him for this assignment.

'It'll be a good-will mission,' Dr Reginald Southwell had decreed, with a twinkle in his eye that his son had supposedly inherited but that his father had insisted he'd lost. 'See how the other half live. Step out of your world of work, work, work for a month, for goodness' sake. You can take off a month for the first time in who knows how long. I promised the matron I'd return and don't want to leave them in the lurch.'

He'd grinned at that. *Poor old Dad.* It dated him well in the past, calling her a matron. The senior nurses were all 'managers' now.

Unfortunate Dad, the poor fellow laid back with his broken arm and his twisted knee. It had been an accident waiting to happen for his father, a man of his advanced age taking random locum destinations while he surfed. But Sam understood perfectly well why he did it.

Sam sighed and turned off the ignition. Too late to back out. He was here now. He climbed out and stretched the kinks from his shoulders. The blue expanse of ocean reminded him how far from home he really was.

Above him towered a lonely white lighthouse silhouetted against the sapphire-blue sky on the big hill behind the hospital. He listened for traffic noise but all he could hear was the crash of the waves on the cliff below and faint beats from a song. *Edge of Nowhere.* Not surprising someone was playing country music somewhere. They should be playing the theme song from *Deliverance.*

He'd told his colleagues he had to help his dad out with his arm and knee. Everyone assumed Sam was living with him while he recuperated. That had felt easier than explaining this.

Lighthouse Bay, a small hamlet on the north coast of New South Wales at the end of a bad road. The locum do-everything doctor. Good grief.

Ellie jumped at the rap on her door frame and turned her face to the noise. She reached out and switched her heroic balladeer off mid-song. The silence seemed to hum as she stared at the face of a stranger.

'Sorry, didn't mean to startle you.' A deep, even voice, quite in keeping with the broad shoulders and impeccable suit jacket, but not in keeping with the tiny, casual seaside hospital he'd dropped into.

Drug reps didn't usually get out this far. That deeply masculine resonance in his cultured voice vibrated against her skin in an unfamiliar way. It made her face prickle with a warmth she wasn't used to and unconsciously her hand lifted and she checked the top button of her shirt. Phew. Force field secure.

Then her confidence rushed back. 'Can I help you?' She stood up, thinking there was something faintly familiar... But after she'd examined him thoroughly she thought, no, he wasn't recognisable. She hadn't seen this man before and she was sure she'd have remembered him.

The man took one step through the doorway but couldn't go any further. Her office drew the line at two chairs and two people. It had always been small but somehow the space seemed to have shrunk to ridiculous tininess in the last few seconds. There was a hint of humour about his silver-blue eyes that almost penetrated the barrier she'd erected but stopped at the gate. Ellie was a good gatekeeper. She didn't want any complications.

Ellie, who had always thought herself tall for a woman, unexpectedly felt a little overshadowed and the hairs on the back of her neck rose gently—in a languorous way, not in fright—which was ridiculous. Really, she was very busy for the next hour until the elderly locum consultant arrived.

'Are you the matron?' He rolled his eyes, as if a private thought piqued him, then corrected himself. 'Director of Nursing?' Smooth as silk with a thread of command.

'Acting. Yes. Ellie Swift. I'm afraid you have the advantage of me.'

The tall man raised his eyebrows. 'I'm Samuel Southwell.' She heard the slight mocking note in his voice. 'The locum medical officer here for the next month.' He glanced at his watch as if he couldn't believe she'd forgotten he was coming. 'Am I early?'

'Ah…'

Ellie winced. Not a drug rep. The doctor. *Oops*.

'Sorry. Time zones. No Daylight Saving for you northerners from Brisbane. Of course. You're only early on our side of the border. I was clearing the decks for your arrival.' She muttered more to herself, 'Or *someone*'s arrival…' then looked up. 'The agency had said they'd filled the temporary position with a Queenslander. I should have picked up the time difference.'

Then the name sank in. 'Southwell?' A pleasant surprise. She smiled with real warmth. 'Are you related to Dr Southwell who had the accident?' At the man's quick nod, Ellie asked, 'How is he?' She'd been worried.

'My father,' he said dryly, 'is as well as can be expected for a man too old to be surfing.' He spoke as if his parent were a recalcitrant child and Ellie felt a little spurt of protectiveness for the absent octogenarian. Then she remembered she had to work with this man for the next month. She also remembered Dr Southwell had two children, and his only son was a consultant obstetrician at Brisbane Mothers and Babies. A workaholic, apparently.

Well, she certainly had someone with obstetric experience for a month. It would be just her luck that they wouldn't have a baby the whole time he was here. Ellie took a breath and plastered on a smile.

First the green frog jumping at her from the door, then the ones croaking outside the window and now the Frog Prince, city-slicker locum who wasn't almost retired, like locums were supposed to be.

'Welcome. Perhaps you'd like to sit down.' She gestured at the only other chair jammed between the storage cupboard and the door frame. She wasn't really sure his legs would fit if he tried to fold into the space.

He didn't attempt to sit and it was probably a good choice.

There was still something about his behaviour that was a little…odd. Did he feel they didn't want him? 'Dr Southwell, your presence here is very much appreciated.'

It took him a couple of seconds to answer and she used them to centre herself. This was her world. No need to be nervous. 'We were very relieved when someone accepted the locum position for the month.'

He didn't look flattered—too flash just to be referred to as 'someone', perhaps?

Ellie stepped forward. Bit back the sigh and the grumbles to herself about how much she liked the old ones. 'Anyway, welcome to Lighthouse Bay. Most people call me Swift, because it's my name and I move fast. I'm the DON, the midwife, emergency resource person and mediator between the medical staff and the nursing staff.' She held out her hand. He looked at her blankly.

What? Perhaps a sense of humour was too much to hope for.

His expression slowly changed to one of polite query. 'Do they need mediation?' He didn't take her hand and she lowered it slowly. Strange, strange man. Ellie stifled another sigh. Being on the back foot already like this was not a good sign.

'It was a joke, sorry.' She didn't say, *'J. O. K. E.,'* though she was beginning to think he might need it spelled out for him. She switched to her best professional mode. The experience of fitting in at out-of-the-way little hospitals had dispatched any pretensions she might have had that a matron was anyone but the person who did all the things other people didn't want to do. It had also taught her to be all things to all people.

Ellie usually enjoyed meeting new staff. It wasn't something that happened too often at their small hospital until Dr Rodgers had retired.

Lighthouse Bay was a place more suited to farming on the hills and in the ocean, where the inhabitants retreated from society, though there were some very trendy boutique industries popping up. Little coffee plantations. Lavender farms. Online boutiques run by corporate women retreating from the cities looking for a sea change.

Which was where Ellie's new clientele for Maternity rose from. Women with considered ideas on how and where they wanted to have their babies. But the town's reliable weekend doctor had needed to move indefinitely for medical treatment and Ellie was trying to hold it all together.

The local farming families and small niche businesses were salt-of-the-earth friendly. She was renovating her tiny one-roomed cottage that perched with two other similar crofts like a flock of seabirds on the cliff overlooking the bay. She'd found the perfect place to forget what a fool she'd been and perfect also for avoiding such a disaster again.

Ellie dreamed of dispensing with the need for doctors at all. But at the moment she needed one supporting GP obstetrician at least to call on for emergencies. Maybe she could pick this guy's brains for ways to circumvent that.

She glanced at the man in front of her—experience in a suit. But not big on conversation. Still, she was tenacious when there was something she wanted, and she'd drag it out of him. Eventually.

In the scheme of things Lighthouse Bay Maternity needed a shake up and maybe she could use him. He'd be totally abreast of the latest best-practice trends, a leader in safe maternity care. He should be a golden opportunity to sway the sticklers to listen to the mothers instead of the easy fix of sending women away.

But, if he wasn't going to sit down then she would deal with him outside the confines of her office. She stood and slipped determinedly past him. It was a squeeze and required body contact. She'd just have to deal with it. 'Would you like a tour?'

Lemon verbena. He knew the scent because at the last conference he'd presented at, all the wives had been raving about the free hotel amenities and they'd made him smell it. It hadn't resonated with him then as it did now. Sam Southwell breathed it in and his visceral response set off rampant alarm bells. He was floundering to find his brain. There was something about the way her buttoned-to-the-neck, long-sleeved white shirt had launched a missile straight to the core of him and exploded, and now the scent of her knocked him sideways as she brushed past.

The way her chin lifted and her cool, grey eyes assessed him and found him wanting, giving him the ultimate hands-off warning when he hadn't even thought about hands on—hadn't for a long time until now—impressed him. Obviously a woman who made up her own mind. She wasn't overawed by him in the least and that was a good thing.

He stared at the wall where 'Swift' had stood a second ago and used all of his concentration to ram the feelings of sheer confusion and lust back down into the cave he used for later thought, and tried to sound at least present for the conversation. She must be thinking he was an arrogant sod, but his brain was gasping, struggling, stumped by the reaction he was having to her.

She was right. Being jammed in this shoebox of an office wasn't helping. What an ironic joke that his father had thought this isolated community would help him return to normal when in fact he'd just fallen off a Lighthouse Bay cliff. His stomach lurched.

He turned slowly to face her as she waited, not quite tapping her foot. He began to feel better. Impatience wasn't a turn-on.

'Yes. A tour would be excellent,' he said evenly. She

must think he was the most complete idiot but he was working to find headspace to fit it all in. And he could work fast.

The place he could handle. Heck, he could do it in his sleep. He had no idea why he was so het up about it. But this woman? His reaction to her? A damnably different kettle of fish. Disturbing. As in, deeply and diabolically disturbing.

'How many beds do you have here?' A sudden picture of Ellie Swift on a bed popped into his head and arrested him. She'd have him arrested, more likely, he thought wryly. He was actually having a breakdown. His dad was right. He did need to learn to breathe.

CHAPTER TWO

SAM HADN'T SLEPT with a woman for years. Not since his wife had died. He hadn't wanted to and in fact, since he'd used work to bury grief and guilt, with all the extra input, his career had actually taken off. Hence, he hadn't had the time to think about sex, let alone act on it.

Now his brain had dropped to somewhere past his waistline, a nether region that had been asleep for years and had just inconveniently roared into life like an express train, totally inappropriate and unwelcome. Good grief. He closed his eyes tightly to try and clear the pictures filling his head. He was an adolescent schoolboy again.

'Are you okay?' Her voice intruded and he snapped his lids open.

'Sorry.' What could he say? He only knew what he couldn't say. *Please don't look down at my trousers!* Instead he managed, 'I think I need coffee.'

She stopped. Dropped her guard. And as if by magic he felt the midwife morph from her as she switched to nurture mode in an instant. No other profession he knew did it as comprehensively as midwives.

'You poor thing. Of course. Follow me. We'll start in the coffee shop. Though Myra isn't here yet. Didn't you stop on the way? You probably rushed to get here.' She shook her head disapprovingly and didn't wait for an answer but bustled him into a small side room that blossomed out into an empty coffee shop with a huge bay window overlooking the gardens.

She nudged him into a seat. Patted his shoulder. 'Tea or coffee?' It had all happened very fast and now his head really was spinning.

'Coffee—double-shot espresso, hot milk on the side,' he said automatically, and she stopped and looked at him.

Then she laughed. Her face opened like a sunburst, her eyes sparkled and her beautiful mouth curved with huge amusement. She laughed and snorted, and he was smitten. Just like that. A goner.

She pulled herself together, mouth still twitching. 'Sorry. Myra could fix that but not me. But I'll see what I can do.'

Sam stared after her. She was at least twelve feet away now and he gave himself a stern talking-to. *Have coffee, and then be* normal. He would try. No—he would succeed.

Poor man. Ellie glanced at the silent, mysterious coffee machine that Myra worked like a maestro and tried to work out how much instant coffee from the jar under the sink, where it had been pushed in disgrace, would equate to a double shot of coffee. She didn't drink instant coffee. Just the weak, milky ones Myra made for her from the machine under protest. Maybe three teaspoons?

He'd looked so cosmopolitan and handsome as he'd said it—something he said every day. She bit back another snuffle of laughter. Classic. *Welcome to Lighthouse Bay.* Boy, were they gonna have fun.

She glanced back and decided he wasn't too worthy of sympathy because it was unfair for a man to have shoulders like that, not to mention a decidedly sinful mouth. And she hadn't thought about sinful for a while. In fact she couldn't quite believe she was thinking about it now. She'd thought the whole devastation of the cruelty of men had completely cured her of that foolishness.

She was going to have to spend the next month with this man reappearing on the ward. Day and night if they were both called out. The idea was more unsettling than she'd bargained for and was nothing to do with the way the ward was run.

The jug boiled and she mixed the potent brew. Best not to think of that now. She needed him awake. She scooped up two Anzac biscuits from the jar with a napkin.

'Here you go.' Ellie put the black liquid down in front of him and a small glass of hot milk she'd heated in the microwave.

He looked at it. Then at her. She watched fascinated as he poured a little hot milk into the mug with an inch of black coffee at the bottom.

He sipped, threw down the lot and then set it down. No expression. No clues. She was trying really hard not to stare. It must be an acquired taste.

His voice was conversational. 'Probably the most horrible coffee I've ever had.' He looked up at her. 'But I do appreciate the effort. I wasn't thinking.' He pushed the cup away. Grimaced dramatically. Shook his whole upper body like a dog shedding water. 'Thank God I brought my machine.'

She wasn't sure what she could say to that. 'Wow. Guess it's going to be a change for you here, away from the big city.'

'Hmm…' he murmured noncommittally. 'But I do feel better after the shock of that.'

She grinned. Couldn't help herself. 'So you're ready for the walk around now?'

He stood up, picked up the biscuits in the napkin, folded them carefully and slipped them into his pocket. 'Let's do it.'

Ellie decided it was the first time he'd looked normal since he'd arrived. She'd remember that coffee trick for next time.

'So this is the ward. We have five beds. One single room and two doubles, though usually we'd only have one woman in each room, even if it's really busy.'

Really busy with five beds? Sam glanced around. Empty rooms. Now they were in with the one woman in the single room and her two-day-old infant. Why wasn't she going home?

'This is Renee Jones.'

'Hello, Renee.' He smiled at the mother and then at the infant. 'Congratulations. I'm Dr Southwell. Everything okay?'

'Yes, thank you, doctor. I'm hoping to stay until Friday, if that's okay. There's four others at home and I'm in no rush.'

He blinked. Four more days staying in hospital after a caesarean delivery? Why? He glanced at Matron Swift, who apparently was unworried. She smiled and nodded at the woman.

'That's fine, Renee, you deserve the rest.'

'Only rest I get,' Renee agreed. 'Though, if you don't mind, could you do the new-born check today, doc, just in case my husband has a crisis and I have to go at short notice?'

New-born check? Examine a baby...himself? He glanced at the midwife. Who did that? A paediatrician, he would have thought. She met his eyes and didn't dispute it so he smiled and nodded. 'We'll sort that.'

Hopefully. His father would be chortling. He could feel Ellie's presence behind him as they left the room and he walked down to the little nurses' alcove and leaned against the desk. It had been too many years since he'd checked a new-born's hips and heart. Not that he couldn't—he imagined. But even his registrars didn't do that. They left it to Paediatrics while the O&G guys did the pregnancy and labour things.

'Is there someone else to do the new-born checks on babies?'

'Sorry.' She shook her head. 'You're it.'

He might have a quick read before he did it, then. He narrowed his eyes at the suspicious quirk of her lips. 'What about you?'

Her hair swished from side to side. He'd never really

had a thing for pony tails but it sat well on her. Pretty. Made him smile when it swayed. He'd faded out again.

'I said,' she repeated, 'I did the online course for well-baby examination but have never been signed off on it. One of those things I've been meaning to do and never got around to.'

Ha. She thought she was safe. 'Excellent. Then perhaps we'd better do the examinations together, and at least by the time I leave we'll both be good at them. Then I can sign you off.'

She didn't appear concerned. She even laughed. He could get used to the way she laughed. It was really more of a chortle. Smile-inducing.

The sound of a car pulling up outside made them both pause. After a searching appraisal of the couple climbing out, she said, 'The charts are in that filing cabinet if the ladies have booked in. Can you grab Josie Mills, please?'

When he looked back from the filing cabinet to the door he could hear the groans but Swift was already there with her smile.

He hadn't seen her move and glanced to where she'd stood a minute ago to check there weren't two of her. Nope. She was disappearing up the hallway with the pregnant woman and her male support as if they were all on one of those airport travellators and he guessed he'd better find the chart.

Which he did, and followed them up the hall.

Josie hadn't made it onto the bed. She was standing beside it and from her efforts it was plain that, apart from him, there'd be an extra person in the room in seconds.

Swift must have grabbed a towel and a pair of gloves as she came through the door, both of which were still lying on the bed, because she was distracted as she tried to help the frantic young woman remove her shorts.

In Sam's opinion the baby seemed to be trying to escape into his mother's underwear but Swift was equal to the task. She deftly encouraged one of the mother's legs out and whipped the towel off the bed and put it between the mother's legs, where the baby seemed to unfold into it in a swan dive and was pushed between the mother's knees into Swift's waiting hands. The baby spluttered his displeasure on the end of the purple cord after his rapid ejection into a towel.

'Good extrication,' Sam murmured with a little fillip of unexpected excitement as he pulled on a pair of gloves from the dispenser at the door. Could that be the first ghost of emotion he'd felt at a birth for a long while? With a sinking dismay it dawned on him that he hadn't even noticed it had been missing.

He crossed the room to assess the infant, who'd stopped crying and was slowly turning purple, which nobody seemed to notice as they all laughed and crowed at the rapid birth and helped the woman up on the bed to lie down.

'Would you like me to attend to third stage or the baby?' he enquired quietly.

He saw Swift glance at the baby, adjust the towel and rub the infant briskly. 'Need you to cut the cord now, John,' she said to the husband. 'Your little rocket is a bit stunned.'

The parents disentangled their locked gazes and Sam heard their indrawn breaths. The father jerked up the scissors Ellie had put instantly into his hand and she directed him between the two clamps as she went on calmly. 'It happens when they fly out.' A few nervous sawing snips from Dad with the big scissors and the cord was cut. Done.

'Dr Southwell will sort you, Josie, while we sort the baby.' Swift said it prosaically and they swapped places as the baby was bundled and she carried him to the resuscitation trolley. 'Come on, John.' She gestured for the father to follow her. 'Talk to your daughter.'

The compressed air hissed as she turned it on and Sam could hear her talking to the dad behind him as automatically he smiled at the mother. 'Well done. Congratulations.'

The baby cried and they both smiled. 'It all happened very fast,' the mother said as she craned her neck toward the baby and, reassured that Swift and her husband were smiling, she settled back. 'A bit too fast.'

He nodded as a small gush of blood signalled the third stage was about to arrive. Seconds later it was done, the bleeding settled, and he tidied the sheet under her and dropped it in the linen bag behind him. He couldn't help a smile to himself at having done a tidying job he'd watched countless times but couldn't actually remember doing himself. 'Always nice to have your underwear off first, I imagine.'

The mother laughed as she craned her neck again

and by her smile he guessed they were coming back. 'Easier.'

'Here we go.' Swift lifted the mother's T-shirt and crop top and nestled the baby skin-to-skin between her bare breasts. She turned the baby's head sideways so his cheek was against his mother. 'Just watch her colour, especially the lips. Her being against your skin will warm her like toast.'

Sam stood back and watched. He saw the adjustments Ellie made, calmly ensuring mother and baby were comfortable—including the dad, with a word here and there, even asking for the father's mobile phone to take a few pictures of the brand new baby and parents. She glanced at the clock. He hadn't thought of looking at the clock once. She had it all under control.

Sam stepped back further and peeled off his gloves. He went to the basin to wash his hands and his mind kept replaying the scene. He realised why it was different. The lack of people milling around.

Swift pushed the silver trolley with the equipment and scissors towards the door. He stopped her. 'Do you always do this on your own?'

She pointed to a green call button. 'Usually I ring and one of the nurses comes from the main hospital to be on hand if needed until the GP arrives. But it happened fast today and you were here.' She flashed him a smile. 'Back in a minute. Watch her, will you? Physiological third stage.' Then she sailed away.

He hadn't thought about the injection they usually gave to reduce risk of bleeding after the birth. He'd somehow assumed it had already been given, but realised there weren't enough hands to have done it, although he could have done it if someone had mentioned it. Someone.

As far as he knew all women were given the injection at his hospital unless they'd expressly requested not to have it. Research backed that up. It reduced postpartum haemorrhage. He'd mention it.

His eyes fell on Josie's notes, which were lying on the table top where he'd dropped them, and he snicked the little wheeled stool out from under the bench with his foot and sat there to read through the medical records. The last month's antenatal care had been shared between his father and 'E Swift'. He glanced up every minute or so to check that both mother and baby were well but nothing happened before 'E Swift' returned.

An hour later Sam had been escorted around the hospital by a nurse who'd been summoned by phone and found himself deposited back in the little maternity wing. The five-minute cottage hospital tour had taken an hour because the infected great toenail he'd been fearing had found him and he'd had to deal with it, and the pain the poor sufferer was in.

Apparently he still remembered how to treat phalanges and the patient had seemed satisfied. He assumed Ellie would be still with the new maternity patient, but he was wrong.

Ellie sat, staring at the nurses' station window in a strangely rigid hunch, her hand clutching her pen six inches above the medical records, and he paused and turned his head to see what had attracted her attention.

He couldn't see anything. When he listened, all he could hear were frogs and the distant sound of the sea.

'You okay?' He'd thought his voice was quiet when he asked but she jumped as though he'd fired a gun past her ear. The pen dropped as her hand went to her chest, as if to push her heart back in with her lungs. His own pulse rate sped up. Good grief! He'd thought it was too good to be true that this place would be relaxing.

'You're back?' she said, stating the obvious with a blank look on her face.

He picked up the underlying stutter in her voice. Something had really upset her and he glanced around again, expecting to see a masked intruder at least. She glanced at him and then the window. 'Can you do me a favour?'

'Sure.' She looked like she could do with a favour.

'There's a green tree frog behind that plant in front of the window.' He could hear the effort she was putting in to enunciate clearly and began to suspect this was an issue of mammoth proportions.

'Yes?'

'Take it away!'

'Ranidaphobia?'

She looked at him and, as he studied her, a little of the colour crept back into her face. She even laughed shakily. 'How many people know that word?'

He smiled at her, trying to install some normality in the fraught atmosphere. 'I'm guessing everyone who's frightened of frogs.' He glanced up the hallway. 'I imagine Josie is in one of the ward rooms. Why don't you go check on her while I sort out the uninvited guest?'

She stood up so fast it would have been funny if he didn't think she'd kill him for laughing. He maintained a poker face as she walked hurriedly away and then his smile couldn't be restrained. He walked over to the pot plant, shifted it from the wall and saw the small green frog, almost a froglet, clinging by his tiny round pads to the wall.

Sam bent down and scooped the little creature into his palm carefully and felt the coldness of the clammy body flutter as he put his other hand over the top to keep it from jumping. A quick detour to the automatic door and he stepped out, tossing the invader into the garden.

Sam shook his head and walked back inside to the wall sink to wash his hands. A precipitous human baby jammed in a bikini bottom didn't faze her but a tiny green frog did? It was a crazy world.

He heard her come back as he dried his hands.

'Thank you,' she said to his back. He turned. She looked as composed and competent as she had when he'd first met her. As if he'd imagined the wild-eyed woman of three minutes ago.

He probably thought she was mad but there wasn't a lot she could do about that now. Ellie really just wanted him to go so she could put her head in her hands and scream with frustration. And then check every other blasted plant pot that she'd now ask to be removed.

Instead she said, 'So you've seen the hospital and your rooms. Did they explain the doctor's routine?'

He shook his head so she went on. 'I have a welcome pack in my office. I'll get it.'

She turned to get it but as she walked away something made her suspect he was staring after her. He probably wasn't used to dealing with officious nursing staff or mad ones. They probably swarmed all over him in Brisbane—the big consultant. She glanced back. He was watching her and he was smiling. She narrowed her eyes.

Then she was back and diving in where she'd left off. 'The plan is you come to the clinic two hours in the morning during the week, starting at eight after your ward round here at seven forty-five. Then you're on call if we need you for emergencies, but most things we handle ourselves. It's a window of access to a doctor for locals. We only call you out for emergencies.'

'So do you do on-call when you're off duty?' He glanced at her. 'You do have off-duty time?'

Ellie blinked, her train of thought interrupted. 'I share the workload with the two other midwives, Trina and Faith. I do the days, Faith does the afternoons and Trina does the nights. We cover each other for on-call, and two midwives from the base hospital come in and relieve us for forty-eight hours on the weekends. We have a little flexibility between us for special occasions.'

'And what do you do on your days off?' She had the feeling he was trying to help her relax but asking about her private life wasn't the way to do that.

She deliberately kept it brief. Hopefully he'd take the hint. 'I enjoy my solitary life.'

She saw him accept the rebuke and fleetingly felt mean. He was just trying to be friendly. It wasn't his fault she didn't trust any man under sixty, but that was the way it was.

She saw his focus shift and his brows draw together, as if he'd just remembered something. 'Syntocinon after birth—isn't giving that normal practice in all hospitals?'

It was a conversation she had with most locums when they arrived—especially the obstetricians like him. 'It's not routine here. We're low risk. Surprisingly, here we're assuming the mother's body has bleeding under control if we leave her well enough alone. Our haemorrhage rate per birth is less than two percent.'

His brows went up again. 'One in fifty. Ours is one in fifteen with active management. Interesting.' He nodded. 'Before I go we'd better check this baby in case your patient wants to go home. I borrowed the computer in the emergency ward and read over the new-born baby check. Don't worry. It all came back to me as I read it.'

He put his hand in his pocket and she heard keys jingle and wondered if it was a habit or he was keen to leave. Maybe he was one of those locums who tried to do as little as possible. It was disconcerting how disappointed she felt. Why would that be? Abruptly she wanted him to go. 'I can do it if you like.'

'No.' He smiled brilliantly at her and she almost stumbled, certainly feeling like reaching for her sunnies. That was some wattage.

Then he said blithely, 'We will practise together.' He picked up a stethoscope and indicated she should get one too.

Ellie could do nothing but follow his brisk pace down the corridor to Renee's room. So he was going to make her copy him. Served her right for telling him she'd done the course.

In Renee's room when he lifted back the sheet, baby Jones lay like a plump, rosy-cheeked sleeping princess all dressed in pink down to her fluffy bloomers. Ellie suppressed a smile. 'Mum's first girl after four boys.'

'What fun,' he murmured.

He started with the baby's chest, listening to both sides of her chest and then her heart. Ellie remembered the advice from the course to start there, because once your examination woke the baby up she might not lie so quietly.

Dr Southwell stepped back and indicated she do the same. Ellie listened to the *lub-dub*, *lub-dub* of a normal organ, the in-and-out breaths that were equal in both lungs, nodded and stood back.

He was right. She'd been putting off asking someone to sign her off on this. Before Wayne, she would have been gung-ho about adding neonatal checks to her repertoire. A silly lack of confidence meant she'd been waiting around for someone else to do it when she should really just have done this instead. After all, when she had the independent midwifery service this would be one of her roles.

By the time they'd run their hands over the little girl, checked her hips didn't click or clunk when tested, that her hand creases, toes and ears were all fine, Ellie was quite pleased with herself.

As they walked away she had the feeling that Dr Southwell knew exactly what she was feeling.

'Easy,' he said and grinned at her, and she grinned

back. He wasn't so bad after all. In fact, he was delightful.

Then it hit her. It had been an action-packed two hours since he'd walked in the door. This physically attractive male had gone from being a stranger standing in her office, to coffee victim, to birth assistant, to frog remover, to midwife's best friend in a couple of hours and she was grinning back at him like a smitten fool. As if she'd found a friend and was happy that he liked her.

Just as Wayne had bowled her over when they'd first met. She'd been a goner in less than an evening. He'd twisted her around his finger and she'd followed him blindly until he'd begun his campaign of breaking her. She'd never suspected the lies.

Oh, yes. Next came the friendly sharing of history, all the warm and fuzzy excitement of mutual attraction, pleasant sex and then *bam*! She'd be hooked. The smile fell off her face.

Not this little black duck.

Ellie dragged the stethoscope from around her neck and fiercely wiped it over with a disposable cleaning cloth. Without looking at Sam, she held out her hand for his stethoscope. She felt it land and glanced at him. 'Thank you. I'll see you tomorrow, then, Dr Southwell.'

She watched his smile fade. Hers had completely disappeared as she'd looked up at him with the same expression she'd met him with this morning. Polite enquiry. He straightened his shoulders and jammed his hand back in his pocket to jingle his keys again.

'Right,' he said evenly. 'I'll go check into my guesthouse.' Without another word, he strode away to the front door and she sagged with relief.

Lucky she'd noticed what she'd been doing before it had gone too far. But at this precise moment she didn't feel lucky. She felt disheartened that she couldn't just enjoy a smile from a good-looking man without getting all bitter, twisted and suspicious about it. Wayne had a lot to answer for.

She did what she always did when her thoughts turned to her horrific marriage that really hadn't been a marriage—she needed to find work to do and maybe Josie or her baby could give it to her.

CHAPTER THREE

THREE NIGHTS LATER, alone in her big oak bed on top of the cliff, Ellie twisted the sheets under her fingers as the dream dragged her back in time. Dragged her all the way back to primary school.

Her respirations deepened with the beginning of panic. The older Ellie knew what the dream Ellie didn't. Her skin dampened.

Then she was back.

To the last day of compulsory swimming lessons she'd used to love. Now school and swimming lessons made her heart hurt. Mummy had loved helping at swimming lessons, had even taught Ellie's class the first two years, but now all they did was remind young Ellie how much she'd lost, because Mummy wasn't there anymore. Daddy had said Mummy would be sad that Ellie didn't like swimming now, but it made her heart ache.

And some of the big boys in primary school were mean to her. They laughed when she cried.

But today was the last day, the last afternoon she'd see the grey toilet block at the swimming pool for this year, and she pushed off her wet swimming costume

*with relief and it plopped to the floor. When she reached
for her towel she thought for a minute that it moved.
Silly. She shook her head and grabbed for it again so
she could dry and get dressed quickly, or she'd be last
in line again and those boys would tease her.*

*Something moved out of the corner of her eye
and then she felt the cold shock as a big, green frog
leaped towards her and landed on her bare chest. She
screamed, grabbed the clammy bulk of it off her slimy
skin and threw it off her chest in mindless revulsion,
then fought with the lock on the change-room door to
escape.*

*The lock jammed halfway. Ellie kept screaming,
then somehow her fingers opened the catch and she
ran out of the cubicle, through the washroom and outside through the door—into a long line of stunned primary school boys who stared and then laughed at the
crying, naked young Ellie until she was swooped on by
a scolding teacher and bundled into a towel.*

*She wanted her mummy. Why couldn't she have her
mummy? It should be her mummy holding her tight and
soothing her sobs. She cried harder, and her racking
sobs seemed to come from her belly, even silencing the
laughing boys...*

Ellie sat bolt upright in bed, the sob still caught in
her throat, and shuddered. She didn't know why frogs
were so linked with her mother's death. Maybe it was
something she'd heard about her mother's car accident,
coupled with her childhood's overwhelming sense of
loss and grief—and of course that incident at the swimming baths hadn't helped—but she couldn't hear a frog

without having that loneliness well back up in her again. It had become the spectre of grief. All through her childhood, whenever she'd been lonely and missed her mother, she'd had the frog nightmare. She'd eventually grown out of it. But, after Wayne, it had started again.

She hadn't had the dream for a while. Not once since she'd moved here a year ago—and she hoped like heck she wasn't going to start having it repeatedly again.

She glanced at the window. It was almost light. She'd have time for a quick walk on the beach before she'd have to come back and shower for work. Find inner peace before the day.

Then she remembered the new doctor. Sam. Day four. One more day and then she'd have the weekend off and wouldn't have to see him. Was that why she'd had the dream? The problem was she liked him. And every day she liked him more. He was lovely to the women. Great with the staff. Sweet to her. And Myra thought the sun shone out of him.

Ellie didn't want to like Sam. Because she'd liked the look of Wayne too, and look where that had ended up.

Of course when she went down to the beach the first person she saw was Dr Sam. Funny how she knew it was him—even from the spectacular rear. Thankfully he didn't see her because he was doing what his father had done—watching the ocean. Sam's broad back faced her as he watched the swells and decided on where to swim. Then he strode into the water.

She walked swiftly along the beach, her flip flops in her hand, waves washing over her toes while she tried not to look as his strong arms paddled out to catch the long run of waves into the shore that delighted the surfers.

She couldn't even find peace on 'her' beach. She stomped up the curve of sand and back again faster than usual, deliberately staring directly in front of her. If she hadn't been so stubborn she would have seen that he was coming in on a wave and would intercept her before she could escape.

He hopped up from the last wave right in front of her. 'Good morning, Ellie Swift.'

She jumped. She glared at his face, then in fairness accepted it wasn't his fault she was feeling crabby. 'Morning, Sam.' Then despite herself her gaze dropped to the dripping magnificence of his chest, his flat, muscled abdomen, strong thighs and long legs, and her breath caught in her throat. Even his feet were masculine and sexy. *My goodness!* Her face flamed and she didn't know where to look.

Sam said, 'The water's a nice temperature,' and she hoped he hadn't noticed her ears were burning.

'Um…isn't it warmer in Queensland?' Her brain was too slow to produce exciting conversation.

He shrugged and disobediently her eyes followed the movement of his splendid shoulders despite her brain telling her to look away. He said, 'Don't know. I haven't swum in the ocean for years.'

That made her pause. Gave her a chance to settle down a little, even wonder why he hadn't been to the beach back home. She needed to get out of here. Create some space. Finally she said, 'Then it's good that you're doing it here. I have your father's surfboard up at my house. I'll arrange to get it to you. I'm late. See you soon.'

Sam stood there and watched her leave. He couldn't help himself and he gave up the fight to enjoy the sight. She had a determined little walk, as if she were on a mission, and trying hard to disguise the feminine wiggle, but he could see it. A smile stretched across his face. Yep. The receding figure didn't look back. He hadn't expected her to. But still, it was a nice way to start the day. Ellie Swift. She was still doing his head in. He had to admit it felt novel to be excited about seeing a woman again. Could it be that after only these few days here he was finding his way to coming back to life?

He hadn't made any progress as far as breaking through her barriers went. Maybe he was just out of practice. But the tantalising thing was that, despite coming from different directions, he sensed the rapport, their commonalities, the fact that inherently they believed in the same values. And he was so damnably attracted to her. He loved watching her at work and would have liked to have seen the woman outside work hours. He didn't understand her aversion to having a friendly relationship with him, but that was her right and he respected it. Thank goodness for work. He'd see her in an hour. He grinned.

Ellie disappeared from sight and Sam strode up the beach to scoop up his towel from the sand. He rubbed his hair exuberantly and stopped. Breathed in deeply.

Felt the early sun on his skin, the soft sea breeze, and he glanced back at the water. The sun shone off the pristine white sand and the ocean glittered. He'd needed this break badly. He hadn't enjoyed the world so much as he had since he'd come here. Life had been grey and closed off to him since Bree's death.

The only light in his long days had been the progression of his patients' pregnancies to viable gestation—so that, even if the babies were born prematurely, it was later in the pregnancy and, unlike his and Bree's children, they had a fighting chance. Other people's surviving children had helped to fill the gaping hole of not having his own family.

Now this place was reminding him there was a whole world outside Brisbane Mothers and Babies. He really should phone his dad and thank him for pushing him to come here.

Thursday night, the nightmare came back again and Ellie woke, breathless and tear-stained, to the phone ringing.

That was a good thing. She climbed out of bed and wiped the sweat from her brow. She grabbed for the phone, relieved to have something else to drive the remnants of the nightmare away. 'Hello?' Her voice was thick and wavered a little.

'Sorry, Ellie. Need you for a maternity transfer. Prem labour.'

Her brain cleared rapidly. 'Be there in five.' That sounded much more decisive. She was in no fit state to walk in the dark but she'd have to. Hopefully a frog wouldn't do her in. Ellie dragged off her high-necked nightdress and pulled on a bra and trousers. Her shirt was in the bathroom and she stumbled through to get it, glancing at her face in the mirror. Almost composed.

But her hands shook as she buttoned her shirt all the way up. Damn nightmares.

She dragged her thoughts away from the dream. 'Who's in prem labour?' Ellie muttered as she ran the comb through her hair. The fringe was sweaty and she grimaced. It wasn't a fashion show and she'd find out who soon enough.

When she reached the hospital, swinging her big torch, she saw the Lexus. Dr Southwell. Trina had called him in as well.

If she thought of him like that, instead of as Sam, there was more distance between them and she was keeping that distance at a premium. That was what she liked about midwifery—nothing was about her. She could concentrate on others, and some 'other' must be well established in labour for Trina to call the doctor as well as Ellie.

She made a speedy pass of the utility vehicle parked at an angle in front of the doors as if abandoned in a hurry. Her stomach sank.

She recognised that car from last year because it had the decals from the fruit market on it.

Marni and Bob had lost their first little girl when she'd been born in a rush, too early. It had all happened too fast for transfer to the hospital for higher level of care, too tragically, and at almost twenty-three weeks just a week too early for the baby to have a hope to survive. Marni had held the shiny little pink body on her skin, stroking her gently, talking through her tears, saying as many of the things she wanted to say to her daughter as she could before the little spirit in such a tiny angel's body gently slipped away.

There had been nothing Ellie could do to help before it was too late except offer comfort. All she'd been able to do was help create memories and mementoes for the parents to take home because they wouldn't be taking home their baby.

Ellie had seen Marni last week. They'd agreed about the fact that she needed to get through the next two weeks and reach twenty-four weeks, how she had to try not to fear that she was coming up to twenty-three weeks pregnant again. That a tertiary hospital couldn't take her that early if she did go into labour. This was too heartbreaking. When Ellie walked into the little birth room her patient's eyes were filled with understandable fear that it was all happening again.

She glanced at Bob chewing his bottom lip, his long hair tousled, his big, tattooed hand gripping one of Marni's while the other hand dug into the bed as if he could stop the world if only it would listen. Old Dr Rodgers would have rubbed their shoulders and said he was so sorry, there was nothing they could do. So what *could* they do?

Marni moaned as another contraction rolled over her.

Sam looked up and saw Ellie, his face unreadable. He nodded at the papers. 'We're transferring. Marni's had nephedipine to stop the contractions and they've slowed a little. I've given IV antibiotics, and prescribed the new treatment we've just started at our hospital for extreme prematurity with some success, but we need to move her out soon before it hots up again. Are you happy to go with her?' There was something darkly intense about the way he said it. As if daring her to stand in his way.

'Of course.' What did he mean? If he was willing to try to save this baby and fight for admission elsewhere, she'd fly to the moon with Marni. But he knew as well as she did that most of the time other hospitals didn't have the capacity to accept extremely premature labour because they wouldn't be able to do anything differently when the baby was born. Too young to live was too young to live. 'They've accepted Marni?'

His face looked grim for a moment. 'Yes,' was all he said, but the look he gave was almost savage, and she blinked, wondering what had happened to him to make him so fierce.

'Ambulance should be here soon,' Trina said. She'd been quietly moving around Marni, checking her drip was secure, removing the used injection trays. She kept flicking sideways glances at Sam, as if he was going to ask her to do something she didn't know how to do, and Ellie narrowed her eyes. Had he done something to undermine her friend's confidence? She'd ask later.

Her gaze fell on the admission notes and she gathered them up to make sure she had the transfer forms filled out. She heard the ambulance pull up outside and didn't have the heart to ask Bob to move his car. They'd manage to work around it with the stretcher.

She rapidly filled in the forms with Trina's notes,

added the times the medications were given and waved to the two female paramedics as they entered.

'Hello, ladies. This is Marni. Prem labour at twenty-three weeks. We need a quick run to the base hospital. I'm coming as midwife escort.'

One of the paramedics nodded at Marni. 'Hello. Twenty-three?' Then a glance at Sam that quickly shifted on. 'Okey-dokey.' She said no more.

Ellie finished the transfer forms and disappeared quickly to pluck the small emergency delivery pack from behind the treatment room door just in case Marni's baby decided otherwise. She sincerely hoped not.

Four hours later Sam watched Ellie for a moment as she filled in paperwork at the desk. He had slipped in the back door from the main hospital and she hadn't seen him arrive, which gave him a chance to study her. Her swanlike neck was bent like the stalk of a tired gerbera. His matron looked weary already and the day had only just started. *His* matron? *Whoa, there.*

But he couldn't help himself asking, 'What time did you get back?' He knew the answer, but it was a conversation opener.

He watched the mask fall across her face. Noted he was far too curious about the cause of that wall around her and kept telling himself to stop wondering. Dark shadows lay beneath her eyes and her skin seemed pale.

She said steadily, 'Five-thirty. It was a lovely sunrise.'

Sam had thought so too—a splash of pink that had blossomed to a deep rose, and then a bright yellow beam soaring out of the cluster of clouds on the horizon over the ocean. The bay itself had already captured him, though he preferred to walk down on the pristine sand of the beach rather than along the cliff tops.

He hadn't been able to sleep after the ambulance had left so he'd sat well back from the edge on the small balcony that looked over the road and across to the headland. He'd spent time on the creakingly slow Internet catching up on his email.

By the time the ambulance had returned past his boarding house to drop Ellie back at the hospital, the sky had been pinking at the edges. She still had an hour before she started work and he'd wondered if she'd go in or if someone else would replace her after a call-out.

Now he knew. He was ridiculously pleased to see her and yet vaguely annoyed that she didn't have backup.

'How was Marni after the trip?'

Her face softened and he leant against the desk. Watched the expressions chase across her face whenever she let the wall down. He decided she had one of the most expressive faces he'd seen when she wasn't being officious. No surprises as to what she was thinking about because it was all out there for him to see.

'Of course, she was upset it was happening again. But the contractions slowed right off.' Concern filled her eyes and he wondered who worried about her while she worried about everyone else. He doubted many people were allowed to worry about her.

Her voice brought him back. 'How do you think she'll go?' She looked at him as if he could pull a miracle out of his hat. It was harder doing it long distance but he'd damn well try. Marni would have the benefit of every medical advance in extreme premature labour from his resources he could muster, every advance he'd worked on for the last four years, or he'd die trying. He wouldn't let *her* down.

'My registrar will arrange for the new drug to be forwarded to Marni and they'll start her on that. The OG at the base hospital will put a cervical suture in tomorrow if she's settled. And she'll stay there in the hospital until she gets to twenty-four weeks, and then after a couple of weeks if everything stays settled she can come home and wait. I'll phone today and confirm that plan with the consultant, and will keep checking until she's settled and sorted.'

'What if she comes in again then? After she comes home?'

Then they would act as necessary. 'We transfer again. By then the baby will be at an age where he or she can fight when we get a bed in a NICU.'

'We didn't get to twenty-four weeks last time.' Worry clouded her eyes.

He resisted the urge to put his hand on her shoulder and tell her to stop worrying. He knew she'd push him away. But the really strange thing was that he even wanted to reach out—this need for connection was new in itself.

He had this! He'd never worried about a response from a woman he was trying to reassure before and wasn't sure how to address it. Or even if he wanted to. Instead he jammed his hand into his pocket and jiggled his keys while he kept his conversation on the subject she was interested in. 'With treatment and persistence, we will this time.'

'Then they're lucky you're here.' Now she looked at him in the way he'd wanted her to since he'd met her. But this time he didn't feel worthy.

But he forced a smile. 'Finally—praise. And now I'm going.' The sooner he did the clinic, the sooner he could come back and check on her.

Ellie watched him walk away. Marni was lucky. She didn't feel so lucky, because a nice guy was the last thing she needed. Why was he being so friendly? She couldn't trust him no matter how nice he was. He'd be here in her face for another three weeks, that was all. Then he'd never come back. Why had his father had to break his arm and send the son?

She closed the file with a snap. Life was out to get her.

She heard the plaintive thought even though she didn't say it out loud and screwed her face up. *Stop whining*, she scolded herself and stood up. *We are lucky to have him. Very lucky.*

But she couldn't help the murky thoughts that were left over from the nightmare. The next day was always a struggle when she'd had the dream. And sometimes it meant she'd get some form of contact from Wayne, as if he was cosmically connected to her dream state so that she was off-balance when he did contact her.

'Hello, my lovely.' Myra's cheerful voice broke into her thoughts and thankfully scattered them like little black clouds blown away by a fresh breeze. Then the smell of freshly brewed coffee wafted towards her from the stylish china mug Myra was holding out for her.

'I hear you had a call-out so I've brought you a kick-start. Though it's not much of a kick.' She grimaced with distaste at the sacrilege of good coffee. 'Half-strength latte.'

Ellie stood up and took the mug. The milky decoration on top looked like a rose this morning. Ellie blew a kiss to the silver-haired lady who always looked quietly elegant in her perfectly co-ordinated vintage outfits. She reminded Ellie of the heroine from a nineteen-twenties detective show, except with silver hair. Myra had said that the only things she'd missed when she'd moved to Lighthouse Bay from Sydney were the vintage clothes shops.

Ellie sipped. 'Oh, yum.' She could hug her friend and not just for the coffee. Myra always made her feel better. 'Just what I need. Thank you. How are you?'

'Fine. Of course.' Myra seated herself gracefully in the nurse's chair beside Ellie. 'I'm going away for the weekend, this afternoon—' she looked away and then back '—and I wondered if you'd feed Millicent.'

'Of course.' Myra's black cat drifted between both crofts anyway and if Myra was away Millicent would miaow at Ellie's front door for attention. 'Easily done. I still have tinned food from last time.'

'Thank you.' Myra changed the subject. 'And how are you going with our new doctor?'

Ellie took another sip. Perfect. 'He seems as popular with the women as old Dr Southwell.'

Myra looked away again and, despite her general

vagueness due to lack of sleep from the night before, Ellie felt the first stirrings of suspicion. 'I know you like him.'

'Sam and I have coffee together every morning. A lovely young man. Very like his father. What do *you* think of him?' There was definitely emphasis on the 'you'.

Myra was not usually so blunt. Ellie's hand stilled as she lifted it to have another sip. 'He seems nice.'

'Nice.' Myra rolled her eyes and repeated, 'Nice,' under her breath. 'He's been here for nearly a week. The man is positively gorgeous and he has a lovely speaking voice.'

Ellie pulled a face. Really! 'So?'

For once Myra appeared almost impatient. 'He's perfect.'

Ellie was genuinely confused. The cup halted halfway to her mouth. 'For what?' Maybe she was just slow today.

Myra's eyes opened wide, staring at her as if she couldn't believe Ellie could be so dense. 'For you to start thinking about young men as other than just partners of the women whose babies you catch.'

'As a male friend, you mean? You seem awfully invested in this doctor.' A horrible thought intruded into her coffee-filled senses. Surely not? 'Did you have anything to do with him coming here?'

Her friend raised one perfectly drawn eyebrow. 'And what influence could I possibly have had?'

It had been a silly thought. Ellie rubbed her brow. She tried to narrow her eyes to show suspicion but suspected she just looked ludicrous. The glint of humour in Myra's eyes made her give up the wordless attempt. So she said instead, 'You seemed pretty cosy with his father last time I saw you.'

Myra ignored that. 'And what have you got against young Dr Sam?' She produced a serviette, and unwrapped a dainty purple-tinted macaroon and placed it precisely on the desk in front of Ellie. She must have retrieved it from the safety of her apron pocket. The sneaky woman knew Ellie couldn't resist them.

'Ooh, lavender macaroon.' Briefly diverted, Ellie put down her cup and picked up the macaroon.

Myra was watching her. She said again, 'He seems a conscientious young man.'

Ellie dragged her eyes from her prize. 'Think I said he was nice.' She looked at the macaroon again. She'd had no breakfast but was planning on morning tea. 'He's too nice.' She picked it up and took a small but almost vicious bite. Sweetness filled her mouth and reminded her how she could be seduced by pretty packages. Wayne had been a pretty package... Her appetite deserted her and she put the remainder of the biscuit back on the plate with distaste.

'Poor macaroon.' There was affectionate humour in Myra's voice. 'Not all men are rotten, you know.'

Ellie nodded. Myra always seemed to know what she was thinking. Like her mother used to know when she'd been a child. Ellie didn't want to risk thinking she was a part of Myra's one-person family. Myra would move on, or Ellie would, and there was no sense in becoming too attached. But she suspected she might be already. It was so precarious. Ellie could manage on her own very well. But back to the real danger—thinking a man could recreate that feeling of belonging. 'I've met many delightful men. Fathers. And grandfathers. The other sort of relationship is just not for me.'

'It's been two years.'

This was persistent, even for Myra. 'Are you match-making? You?' She had another even more horrific thought. 'Did you and old Dr Southwell cook this up between you?'

'I hardly think Reginald—whom I would prefer you didn't call *old* Dr Southwell—would break his arm just to matchmake his son with the midwife at the hospital.'

Ellie narrowed her eyes. 'So neither of you discussed how poor Ellie and poor Sam could be good for each other?'

Myra threw up her hands in a flamboyant gesture that was a little too enthusiastic to be normal. 'For good-ness' sake, Ellie. Where do you get this paranoia?'

She hadn't answered the question, Ellie thought warily, but she couldn't see why the pair of them would even think about her that way. She was being silly. Still, she fervently hoped Dr Southwell Senior hadn't men-tioned her as a charity case to his son. That would be too embarrassing and might just explain his friendli-ness. A charity case...please, no.

Myra left soon after and Ellie watched her depart with a frown. Thankfully, she was diverted from her uncomfortable suspicions when a pregnant woman pre-sented for her routine antenatal visit, so the next hour was filled. Ellie liked to add an antenatal education component if the women had time. She was finding it helped the women by reducing their apprehension of labour and the first week with the baby after birth.

Then a woman on a first visit arrived to ask about birthing at Lighthouse Bay instead of the base hospital where she'd had her last baby and Ellie settled down with her to explain their services. Word was getting out, she thought with satisfied enthusiasm.

The next time Ellie turned around it was lunchtime and she rubbed her brow where a vague headache had settled. She decided lack of sleep was why she felt a little nauseated and tried not to worry that it could be one of the twelve-hour migraines that floored her coming on.

Renee's husband arrived, armed with a bunch of flowers, and with their children hopping and wriggling like a box full of field mice, to visit Mum. The way his eyes darted over the children and the worried crease in his forehead hinted that Renee might decide to leave her safe cocoon early and return to running the family.

Ellie suspected the new mum was becoming bored with her room anyway and could quite easily incorporate her new princess into the wild household and still manage some rest.

It proved so when a relieved father came back to the desk to ask what they needed to do before discharge.

'It's all done. Renee has a script for contraception, baby's been checked by the doctor, and she's right to go.'

The relief in his face made Ellie smile at him despite the pain now throbbing in her head. 'Did you have fun with the kids, Ned?'

He grimaced. 'Not so much on my own. They've been good, but…'

Ned carried the smallest, a little carrot-topped boy, and an armful of gift bags out of the ward doorway with a new purpose and possibly less weight on his shoulders. Two more toddlers and a school-aged boy carrying flowers appeared from down the ward, with Renee bringing up the rear with her little princess in her arms, a wide smile on her face.

The foyer in front of the work station clamoured with young voices, so Ellie missed Sam as he returned from clinic and stood at the side of the room.

'Thank you, both,' Renee said. 'It was a lovely holiday.' She was looking past Ellie to the man behind her.

Ellie turned in time to see her new nemesis grin back. She didn't have the fortitude to deal with the 'charity' overtones left from Myra, so she turned quickly back again.

'I think you may be busy for a while,' Sam said to the mother.

Renee nodded calmly and then winked at Ellie. Lowering her voice, she confided, 'It does Ned good to have them for a day or two—lets him see what it's like to be home all day with the darlings in case he's forgotten.'

CHAPTER FOUR

THE AUTOMATIC DOORS closed behind the big family and they both watched them disappear. Sam turned and Ellie saw that flashing smile again. 'Imagine juggling that mob! It wouldn't be dull.'

There was a pause but she didn't say anything. She couldn't think of anything to say, which was peculiar for her, and had a lot to do with the fact that her vision had begun to play up. Small flashes of light were exploding behind her eyes. Migraine.

He filled the silence. 'Do you enjoy watching the women go home with their new babies?'

'Of course. That's a silly question!' He was looking at her with a strange, thoughtful intensity but she was too tired to work it out. She really wasn't in the mood for games. 'Don't you?'

'It isn't about me.' He paused, as if something was not right. 'I'm wondering why a young, caring woman is running a little two-bit operation like this in a town that's mostly populated with retirees and young families.'

Go. Leave me so I can will this headache away. Her

patience stretched nearly to breaking point. 'Me?' She needed to sit and have a cup of tea and maybe a couple of headache tablets. 'Our centre is just as efficient as any other centre of care. What's the difference between here and the city? Are you a "tertiary hospital or nothing" snob?'

'No.' He looked at her. '"Tertiary hospital" snob?'

'Size isn't everything, you know.'

He raised his brows at her. 'I'm very aware of that. Sorry. I was just wondering when you were going to be one of these women coming in to have your perfect little family.'

That stung because she knew it wasn't a part of any future waiting for her on the horizon. Though it should have been. 'There is no perfect little family.'

She looked at him coldly, because abruptly the anger bubbled and flared and her head hurt too much to pretend it wasn't there. 'Where's your perfect little family? Where are your children?'

Lordy, that had sounded terrible. She felt like clapping her hand over her mouth but something about his probing was getting right up her nose.

He winced but his voice was calm. 'Not everyone is lucky enough to have children. I probably won't have any, much to my father's disgust. You're a midwife with empathy pouring out of every inch of you, just watching other women become mothers.'

Easily said. She closed her eyes wearily. 'There's no difference between you and me.'

He didn't say anything and when she opened her eyes he shook his head slowly. 'I saw the way you looked at

Renee's baby. And Josie's. As if each one is a miracle that still amazes you.'

'And you?' She waved a listless hand. 'There's nothing there that spells "misogynist and loner".'

He physically stepped back. 'I really shouldn't have started this conversation, should I?'

'No.' She stood up and advanced on him. She even felt the temptation to poke him in the chest. She didn't. She never poked anyone in the chest. But the pressure in her head combined with the emotion, stresses, and fear from the last few days—fear for Marni's baby, her horrible fear of frogs and this man who was disrupting her little world—and she knew she had a reason to be running scared. Add lack of sleep and it wasn't surprising she had a migraine coming on like a fist behind her eyes.

Stop it, she told herself. She closed her eyes again and then looked down. She said with weary resignation, because she knew she was being unreasonable, 'Sorry. Can you just go?'

She didn't know how she could tell he was looking at her despite the fact she was considering his shoes. His voice floated to her. 'I'm sorry. My fault for being personal.'

That made her look up. He actually did look apologetic when it was she who was pouring abuse like a shrew and had lost it. Her head pounded. She felt like she was going to burst into tears. Actually, she felt sick.

She bolted for the nearest ladies' room and hoped like hell there wasn't a frog in the sink.

Afterwards, when she'd washed her face and didn't

feel much better, she dragged herself to the door, hoping he had gone. Of course, he hadn't; he had waited for her outside in the corridor.

'You okay?'

'Fine.' The lights behind her eyes flickered and then disappeared into a pinpoint of light. She swayed and everything went dim and then black.

Sam saw the colour drain from Ellie's face, the skin tone leeching from pink to white in seconds. His brain noted the drama of the phenomenon while his hands automatically reached out and caught her.

'Whoa there,' he muttered, and scooped her up. She was lighter than he expected, like a child in his arms, though she wasn't a tiny woman with her long arms and neck that looked almost broken, like a swan's, as she lay limp in his embrace.

Unfortunately there was no denying the surge of protective instinct that flooded him as he rested her gently on the immaculate cover of the nearest bed. He'd really have to watch that. He was already thinking about her too much when he wasn't here, when in fact it was unusual for him to feel anything for anybody at all.

Her damn collar was buttoned to the neck again—how on earth did she stand it?—and he undid the first and second buttons and placed his finger gently against her warm skin to feel the beating of her carotid artery.

Her skin was like silk and warmer than he expected. She must be brewing something. Sudden onset, pallor, faint… He didn't know her but she hadn't struck him as the fainting type… Before he could decide what to do she groaned and her eyelids fluttered. Then she was staring up at him. Her blue eyes were almost violet. Quite beautiful.

'Where am I?'

He glanced at the sign on the door. 'Room one.'

She drew her dark brows together impatiently. 'How did I get here?'

'You fainted.'

The brows went up. 'You carried me?' He quite liked her brows. Amusing little blighters. Her words penetrated and he realised he was going mad again. She was the only one who did that to him.

He repeated. 'You fainted. I caught you. Can't have you hitting your head.' She struggled to sit up and he helped her. 'Slowly does it.'

'I never faint.'

He bit back the smile. 'I'm afraid you can't say that any more.'

She actually sagged a little at that and he bit back another smile. Behind her now not-so-tightly buttoned collar, which she hadn't noticed he'd unbuttoned, she wasn't the tough matron she pretended to be. She was cute, though he'd die rather than tell her that. He could just imagine the explosion. 'Stay there. I'll get you some water.' He paused at the door. 'Did you eat breakfast this morning?'

She passed a hand over her face. 'I can't remember.'

'I'll get you water and then I'll get you something to eat.' He could already tell she was going to protest. 'You made me coffee on Monday. I can do this for you. It'd be too embarrassing to fall into my arms again, right?'

She subsided. The fact she stayed put actually gave him a sense of wicked satisfaction that made his lips curve. *Tough luck. My rules this time.*

With a stab of painful guilt that washed away any amusement, he remembered he hadn't looked after Bree enough, hadn't been able to save her, or his own premature children. But maybe he could look after Ellie—at least for the month he was here.

He heard her talking to herself as he left. 'I'll have to get a relief midwife to come in.'

He walked out for the water but didn't know where to get the glass from. He'd have to ask her, so was back a few seconds later.

She was still mumbling. 'I'll be out for at least twelve hours.'

He stopped beside the bed. 'Does your head hurt?'

She glared at him. 'Like the blazes. I thought you were getting water.'

'Cups?'

'Oh. Paper ones on the wall beside the tap.'

Ellie closed her eyes as Sam left the room. How embarrassing! She hadn't fainted in her life and now she'd done it in front of a man she'd particularly wanted to maintain professional barriers with. She'd never fainted with a migraine before. Oh, goody, something new to add to the repertoire.

Where was Myra when she needed her? She wished Sam would just leave. Though when he returned with the water she gulped it thirstily.

'Go easy. I don't have a bowl or know where they live.'

Ellie pulled the paper cup away from her lips. He

was right. She was still feeling sensitive but her throat was dry and raw. She sank back against the pillows. She'd have to strip this bed because she'd crumpled it.

Maybe the weekend midwife could come early. This afternoon. She'd meant to go shopping for food and now she knew she didn't have the energy. She'd just hole up until tomorrow, when she'd be fine. The thoughts rolled around in her head, darting from one half-considered worry to another.

'Stop it.'

She blinked. 'Stop what?'

'Trying to solve all the logistical problems you can see because you do everything around here.'

'How do you know I'm thinking that?' It came out more plaintively than she'd expected. How did he know she did do most things?

He looked disgustingly pleased with himself. 'Because the expressions on your face mirror your every thought. Like reading a book.'

Great. Not! 'Well, stop reading my book.'

'Yes, ma'am.' But his eyes said, *I quite like it.*

She reached down into her fast fading resources. 'If you would like to help, could you please ask Myra to come around from the coffee shop?'

'Myra has left for the weekend. Going away somewhere. There's a young woman holding the fort, if you would like a sandwich.'

Her heart sank. Clarise… Clarise could make toast, which might help, but she'd have to do everything else herself. 'Already? Damn.'

'Can I do something for you?' He spread his hands. 'I've done all my homework.'

Ellie looked at him. Tall, too handsome, and relaxed with one hand in his pocket. Leaning on the door jamb as if he had all the time in the world. She had a sudden picture of him in his usual habitat surrounded by a deferential crowd of students, the man with all the answers, dealing with medical emergencies with swift decision and effectiveness. She had no right to give this man a hard time. Her head throbbed and the light was hurting her eyes. Now she felt like crying again. Stupid weakness.

His voice intruded on her thoughts and there was understanding in his eyes, almost as if he knew how much she hated this. 'You look sad. Is it so bad to have to ask me for help?'

My word, it is. 'Yes.'

Of course he smiled at that. 'Pretend I'm someone you hired.'

'I don't have to pretend. I did hire you.'

He laughed at that. 'Technically the administration officer hired me.'

'That would be me.'

'So what would you like me to do?'

She sat up carefully and swung her legs over the bed. He came in closer as if to catch her if she fell. It was lucky, because her head swam and she didn't want to smack the linoleum with her face.

'Just make sure I make it to the desk and the phone and the rest I can manage. Maybe you could stay in case anyone else comes in while we wait for my replacement.

Even I can see there's no use me being here if I can't be trusted not to fall on my face.'

'Especially when it's far too pretty a face to fall on.'

She looked at him. Narrowed her eyes. 'Don't even go there.'

He held up his hands but she suspected he was laughing at her again. Together they made their way over to the desk and with relief she sank into her usual chair. She reached into her handbag, pulled out her sunglasses and put them on. The pain from the glare eased.

It only took an hour for her replacement to arrive but it felt like six. She just wanted to lie down. In fact her replacement's arrival had been arranged faster than expected, and was only possible because the midwife had decided to spend an extra day at Lighthouse Beach, on the bay, before work.

Ellie had sipped half a cup of tea. She'd taken two strong headache tablets and really wanted to sink into her bed. Standing at the door with her bag over her arm, she wasn't sure how she was going to get up the hill to her croft.

'I'll drive you.'

He was back. And he'd read her mind again. She wished he'd stop doing that. He'd left for an outpatient in the other part of the hospital after Ellie had assured him she'd be fine until the relief midwife arrived and she had been hoping to sneak away.

She'd have loved to say no. 'If you don't mind, I'll have to take you up on that offer.'

'So graciously accepted,' he gently mocked.

He was right. But she didn't care. All she could think about was getting her head down and sinking into a deep sleep.

He ushered her to his car, and made sure she was safely tucked in before he shut the door.

'Do you always walk to work?'

'It's only at the top of the hill.' She rested her head back against the soft leather headrests and breathed in the aroma of money. Not something she'd sniffed a lot of in her time. 'I always walk except in the rain. It's a little slippery on the road when it's wet.'

'Did you come down in the dark, last night?'

She didn't bother opening her eyes. 'I have a torch.'

'You should drive down at night.'

Spare me. 'It's two hundred and fifty metres.'

He put the car into gear, turned up the steep hill and then turned a sharp left away from the lighthouse, onto the road with three cottages spaced privately along the headland. 'Who owns the other ones?'

'I'm in the first, Myra is the end one and the middle one is Trina, so try not to rev your engine because she's probably sleeping.'

'I'll try not to.' Irony lay thick in his voice. He parked outside the first cottage and turned the car off. She'd hoped she could just slip out and he'd drive away.

They sat for a moment with the engine ticking down. Ellie's headache had reached the stage where she didn't want to move and she could feel his glance on her. She didn't check to see if she was imagining it. Then she heard his door open and the car shifted as he got out.

When her door opened the cool salt air and the crash

from the waves on the cliffs below rushed in and she revived a little.

Sam spoke slowly and quietly as if to a frightened child. 'If you give me the key, I could open the door for you?'

'It's not locked.'

'You're kidding me?' The words hung in disbelief above her. Apparently that concept wasn't greeted with approval. He said in a flat voice, 'Tonight it should be.'

She held her head stiffly, trying not to jar it, and turned in the seat. She locked it at night but the daytime was a test for herself. She would not let her life be run by fear. 'Thank you for the lift.'

He put out his hand and Ellie wearily decided it was easier just to take it and use his strength to achieve a vertical position. Her legs wobbled a bit. He hissed out a breath and picked her up.

'Hey.'

'Hey, what?' A tinge of impatience shone through.

'You'll fall down if you try to walk by yourself.'

And then she was cradled tight against his solid warm chest and carried carefully towards her door. He leant her against the solid wood and turned the handle, then they were both inside.

Sam had expected the inside to be made up of smaller compartments but it was a big room that held everything. There was a tiny kitchen at the back with a chimney over the big, old wood-burner stove. A shiny gas stove and refrigerator stood next to it and a scrubbed wooden table and four chairs.

A faded but beautiful Turkish rug drew the sections of the home together in the middle where it held a soft cushioned sofa with a coffee table in front that faced the full-length glass doors out to sea. Bookshelves lined the rear walls and a couple of dark lighthouse paintings were discernible in the corners. There was a fireplace. A big red-and-white Malibu surfboard leant against the wall. His father's. He looked at it for a moment then away.

A patchwork-quilted wooden bed sat half-hidden behind a floral screen, pastel sheets and towels were stacked neatly in open shelves and across the room was a closed door which he presumed was the bathroom. Nothing like the sterile apartment he'd moved into after Bree's death and where he'd never unpacked properly.

The bed, he decided, and carried her across and placed her gently on the high bed's quilt.

'Come in,' she said with an exhausted edge to her voice as he put her down. Talk about ungrateful.

He stepped back and looked at her. She looked limp, with flushed spots in her pale face. Still so pale. Pale and interesting. She was too interesting and she was sick. He told himself she was a big girl. But that didn't mean he liked leaving her. 'Can I make you a cup of tea before I go?'

'No, thank you.'

He sighed and glanced at the room behind him again, as if seeking inspiration. He saw his dad's surfboard again. He'd said the midwife was minding it for him and that Sam should try it out. Maybe he would one day. But not today. It would be a good reason to come back.

He glanced through the double-glazed doors facing the ocean and he could imagine it would be a fabulous sight on wild weather days. But it was also too high up and exposed for him to feel totally comfortable. And she lived here alone.

He thought about the other two crofts and their occupants. It was a shame Myra was away.

'How about I leave a note for Trina and ask her if she'll check on you later?' *Before she goes to work for the night and leaves you up here all alone*, he added silently.

'No, thank you.' Her eyes were shut and he knew she was wishing him gone.

She was so stubborn. Why did he care? But he did. 'It's that or I'll come back.'

She opened her eyes. 'Fine. Leave a note for Trina. Ask if she'll drop in just before dark. I'll probably be fine by then.'

Sounded reasonable. Then she could lock the door.

That was all he could do. He saw her fight to raise her head and tilt it meaningfully at the door and he couldn't think of any other reason to stay.

He walked to the sink. Took a rinsed glass from the dish rack and filled it with water. Carried it back without a word and put it beside her. Then he felt in his pocket, retrieved his wallet and took out a business card. 'That's my mobile number. Ring me if you become seriously ill. Or if you need medication. I'll come. No problem.'

Then he tore himself away and shut the door carefully behind him, grimacing to himself that he couldn't lock it. Anybody could come up here and just waltz in while she was sleeping. Surely she locked it at night?

When he went next door and wrote on another of his business cards, he decided he should at least see if he could hear if Trina was awake. He walked all the way around the little house. Because he could. It was just like Ellie's, though there was a hedge separating them from each other and the cliff path that ran in front of the houses.

Anybody could walk all the way around these houses. The view was impressively dramatic, except he didn't enjoy it. The little crofts clung to the edge of the cliff like fat turtles and the narrow walkway against the cliff made his mouth dry.

At least the dwellings looked like they wouldn't blow off into the sea. They were thick-walled, with shutters tied back until needed for the really wild weather. Daring the ocean winds to try and shift them.

He was back at the front door again. No sounds from Trina's. She could sleep right through until tonight. He'd have to come back himself. Before dark, like Ellie had said.

Sam drove back down the hill to his guesthouse. He let himself in the quaint side entrance with his key and up the stairs to his balcony room. He threw the keys from his pocket onto the dresser, opened the little fridge, took out a bottle of orange juice and sipped it thoughtfully as he walked towards the windows.

She'd sleep for a while. He wished she'd let him stay but of course she'd sleep better without him prowling around. He knew it was selfish because if he'd been there he wouldn't have had to worry about her. Being away from her like this, he couldn't settle.

He felt a sudden tinge of remorse that made him grimace, an admission of unfaithfulness to Bree's memory. It hung like a mist damning him, because he was so fixated on Ellie, but also underneath was a little touch of relief that he was still capable of finally feeling something other than guilt and devastation.

His father would be pleased. He'd say it was time to let go of the millstone of his guilt over Bree, that it was holding him back and not doing the memory of their relationship justice. Was it time finally to allow himself the freedom to feel something for someone else?

His heartbeat accelerated at the thought but he told himself it would all be fine. He was only here for another few weeks, after all, and he'd be heading home after that. Strangely, the time limit helped to make him feel more comfortable with his strange urge to look after Ellie.

The sun shone and turned the blue of the ocean to a brilliant sapphire and he decided he'd go for another swim. No wonder his dad had raved about this place. Then he'd go back and check on Ellie after he'd showered.

CHAPTER FIVE

ELLIE HEARD SAM close the door when he left. She pulled the blanket up higher to calm the shudders that wracked her body. He'd been very good, and she should have said thank you, but the headache had built steadily again. It was easier to breathe in and out deeply, to make it go away and wait for sleep to claim her, and then maybe she'd wake up and all this would just have been a bad dream. Her hair was heavy on her forehead and she brushed it away. She was too disinclined to move to take a sip of the water he'd put there. Mercifully, everything faded.

When she fell asleep she had the nightmare.

She moaned because her head hurt as well.

Slowly the afternoon passed. As evening closed in the nightmares swirled around her, mixed themselves with imagined and remembered events.

But while she slept her troubled sleep there were moments when she felt safe. Moments when she felt a damp, refreshing washcloth on her brow. She dreamt she sipped fluid and it was cool and soothing on her throat. Even swallowed some tablets.

The bad dream returned. Incidents from her time with Wayne mixed in with it. Incidents from their spiral downhill flashed through her mind: cameos of her hurt and bewilderment when he'd barely spoken to her, mocked and ridiculed her...her phobia, her need for nurturing. Screaming he never wanted a family that time she'd thought she was pregnant. *All* she wanted was a family.

The dream flashed to the afternoon at the swimming pool again and she moaned in the bed. Twisted the sheets in her hand.

She fought the change room door. Ran into the boys outside...

She sobbed. She sobbed and sobbed.

'It's okay, sweetheart. Stop. My God. It's okay.'

The words were seeping through the horror and the mists of sweat and anguish. Sam's voice. His arms were around her. Her head was tucked into his chest, her hair was being stroked.

'Ellie. Wake up. It's a dream. Wake up!'

Ellie opened her eyes and a shirt button was pressing into her nose. A man's shirt.

'It's okay.' It was Sam's voice, Sam's big hands rubbing her back. A man's scent. So it must be Sam's shirt. Sam?

She was still foggy but clearing fast. What was he doing here? She pushed him away.

His hands moved back and his body shifted to the edge of the bed from where he'd reached for her. 'That's some nightmare.'

She brushed her damp hair out of her face, muttered, 'Why are you here?'

'Because Trina is at work, Myra's away and I wasn't sure you wouldn't get worse.'

He raised his brows and shook his head. 'You did get worse. It's almost midnight and you've been mumbling and tossing most of the evening. If you didn't get better soon I was going to admit you and put up a drip.'

Dimly she realised her head didn't hurt any more but it felt dense like a bowling ball, and just as heavy. It would clear soon, she knew that, but she couldn't just lie here crumpled and teary. The tendrils of the nightmare retreated and she wiped her face and shifted herself back up the bed away from him, pushing the last disquieting memories back into their dark place in her brain at the same time.

As she wriggled, he reached and flipped the pillows over and rearranged them so she could sit up.

Then he rose. She wasn't sure if that was better because now he towered over her, and it must have shown on her face, because he moved back and then turned away to walk to the kitchen alcove.

He switched on the jug, turned his head towards her and said quietly, 'Would you like a drink? Something hot?'

Her mouth tasted like some dusty desert cavern. She'd kill for a cup of tea. Maybe it wasn't so bad he was here. 'Yes, please. Tea?' She sounded like a scared kitten. She cleared her throat, mumbled, 'Thank you,' in a slightly stronger voice. She glanced down at her crumpled uniform but it was gone and she was in her bra and pants. Her face flushed as she yanked the covers up to her neck.

'You took off my shirt and trousers?'

'You were tangled in them. Sweating. I asked you and you said yes.'

She narrowed her eyes at him. 'I don't remember that.'

He came back with the mug of tea. 'I'm not surprised. You've been barely coherent. If that's a migraine, I hope I don't get one. Nasty.'

'I can't believe you undressed me.'

He waggled his brows. 'I left the essentials on.'

Her face grew even hotter. *Cheeky blighter.*

He put the tea down beside her. 'Do you have a dressing gown or something I can get you?'

'In the bathroom, hanging behind the door.' She took a sip and it tasted wonderful. Black. Not too hot. He must have put cold water in it so she didn't burn her tongue. That was thoughtful. While she sipped he poked his head into the little bathroom and returned with her gown.

Speaking of the bathroom... She needed to go, and imagined taking a shower. Oh, yes...that wouldn't go astray either if she could stay standing long enough to have it. The idea of feeling fresh and clean again grew overpoweringly attractive.

'Um... If you turn around, I'd like to get up.'

He considered her and must have decided she had more stamina than she thought she had because he nodded.

'Sure.' He crossed his arms and turned around, presenting his broad back to her. She shifted herself to the edge of the bed and swung her legs out. For a moment the room tilted and then it righted.

'You okay?' His voice came but he didn't turn. At least he played fair.

'Fine.' She took another breath, reached down and snatched clean underwear and a nightgown from the drawer beside her bed and stood up on wobbly legs. By the time she shut the door behind her in the bathroom, she was feeling better than she expected. *Good tea.*

By the time she showered and donned her night-dress and dressing gown again, she was feeling almost human.

When she opened the door the steam billowed into the room and for a moment she thought the cottage was empty. But he was sitting on the sofa with his head resting back and she remembered he'd been here all evening.

Guilt swamped her and she padded silently towards him to see if he'd fallen asleep. His eyes were definitely open as she tipped her head down to peer at him. There was a black cat at his feet. She'd forgotten Myra's cat.

'Did you feed Millicent?'

He patted the sofa seat beside him. 'Yes. She had sardines. You look better. I'll go soon, but first tell me about your dream.'

Instinctively she shook her head but she saw there were two cups and her teapot on the low table in front of him. She could do another civilised cup of tea after he'd been so good.

She remembered his arms, comforting her, making

her feel safe, as though she were finding refuge from the mental storm she'd created from her past, and her cheeks heated.

She pulled her dressing gown neckline closer and sat gingerly a safe distance along the sofa from him. 'Thank you for looking after me,' she said, and even to her own ears it sounded prim and stilted.

'You. Are. Very. Welcome.' He enunciated slowly as if to a child, and she glanced at him to see if he was making fun of her. There was a twinkle, but mostly there was genuine kindness without any dramatics.

She glanced back at the bed. It was suspiciously tidy. And a different colour. 'Did you change the sheets?'

'I did. The damp ones are on the kitchen chair. Where is your laundry in your little hobbit house?'

She had to smile at that. 'Does that make me a hobbit?'

'If so, you're a pretty little hobbit.'

'That's a bit personal between a doctor and a patient, isn't it?'

He waggled his finger, making the point. 'You are my friend. Definitely not my patient. I'm glad I didn't have to admit you.'

She wasn't quite sure how to take that and then he said very quietly, 'But listening to you suffer through those dreams was pretty personal. You nearly broke my heart.'

She moved to rise but he touched her arm. 'As your non-doctor friend, can I say I think now is a really good time for you to share your nightmares. Stop the power they have over you.'

She shivered but she subsided and glanced around the room. Anywhere but at him. The dish rack was empty. No dirty dishes. Distractions would be good. 'Have you eaten?'

He patted his flat belly. 'I ate early, before I came. In case I needed to stay. But I've helped myself to your tea.'

His arm came out and quite naturally he slid it around her waist. Bizarrely her body remembered that feeling, although her memory didn't, as he pulled her snug up against his firm hip. 'Tell me. Was it frogs?'

She shuddered. 'It's a long story.'

She felt him shrug under her. 'We have many hours until morning.'

She looked at him. 'It's not that long a story.'

He chuckled quietly, and it was an 'everything is normal even though we are sitting like this in the dark' sound, and despite the unconventional situation she felt herself relax against him.

'I'm all ears,' he said.

She turned her head and looked at him. 'They're big but I wouldn't say you are *all* ears.'

'Stop procrastinating.'

So she told him about the frog in the change room at school and the boys and, hearing it out loud for the second time since the therapist, she felt some of the power of it drain away. It was a little girl's story. Dramatic at the time but so long ago it shouldn't affect her now. In the cool quiet of the morning, with waves crashing distantly, she could accept that the frog was long dead and the little boys were all probably daddies with their own children now. That quite possibly Sam's idea of repeating it now could have merit because it seemed to have muted its power.

He said thoughtfully, 'If you could go back in time, to the morning before that, if you could prepare that little girl in some way, how could you help that young Ellie? What would you tell her?'

She thought about that. Wondered about what the misty memory of her mother might have said to her as a little girl if she had known it was going to happen.

'The frog is more frightened than you are?' The words came from some distant place she couldn't recognise but with them came a gentle wave of comfort. Relief, even. She thought of the child that she had been all those years ago. Sad eyes under the pony tail, freckles, scuffed knees from climbing tress to get away from teasing boys.

'If I had the chance. That might help her,' she said, and looked at Sam.

Sam nodded and squeezed her shoulder. 'So it was the same dream. Over and over?'

She looked at the floor. 'The other one's an even longer story and I don't think I'm up to that tonight.'

He looked at her and she shifted under his scrutiny. 'Okay. So, will you invite me back?'

Why on earth would he want to come back after these last exhausting hours? 'For frog stories?'

He shrugged again. 'There doesn't have to be stories. Can't I come back because I'd like to come back?'

She felt the shift in herself. Felt the weight of his arm, suddenly unbearable. Could almost imagine the bricks all slamming together between them, creating a wall like a scene in a fantasy movie.

Her voice was flat. Different from what it had sounded like only minutes ago. There was no way he could miss the change. 'You live in Brisbane. Your world is different to mine. We'll never be friends.' She tried to shrug off his arm and after a moment he let it fall. He shifted his body away to give her space and she appreciated his acceptance.

He looked at her and suddenly she felt the wall go up from him as well. Contrarily, she immediately wanted the openness that had been there before. Served her right.

But his voice was calm. It hadn't changed like hers had. 'I disagree. Friends can be made on short acquaintance. I'd like to come back later today and just check you're okay.'

Was he thick? Or just stubborn? How did she say no after he'd sat up here and minded her? Made her tea? After all, he would be gone in a few weeks. 'Did you give me water and wipe my face?'

He nodded. 'I didn't think you'd remember that. You weren't awake.'

'There were parts of the dream that weren't all bad.' She looked at him. 'It gets cool here in the night. Were you warm enough?'

He gestured to the throw folded at the end of the sofa. 'If somebody had visited, they would have found a very strange man wearing a blanket.'

She digested that and said simply, 'Thank you.' She

shook her head because she couldn't understand the mystery of his actions. 'Why did you stay?'

He shrugged. As if it was nothing special. No mystery for him. Lucky him. 'Because I didn't know if you would actually ring me if you needed help. You might have needed someone and I couldn't see anyone else coming.'

He'd stayed out of pity. The thought sat like dirty oil in the bottom of her stomach. She shouldn't have been surprised, because she was alone. No family. No husband. 'So you felt sorry for me.'

Sam compressed his lips as if being very careful about what came out of his mouth. She could live with the truth as long as it *was* the truth.

'I had sympathy for you, yes. You were unwell. I hope you would have done it for me if the roles had been reversed.'

She thought about that. Narrowed her eyes. 'Maybe. That's a sneaky way of wriggling out of the "pity" accusation.'

He sighed. Stood up. 'I'm tired. And I might yet get called out. I'm going home. I'll drop back before lunch and see how you are.'

'You could just call me on the phone to check on me.'

He studied her. 'I'll drop back after I do a round at the hospital.'

She stood up, careful to keep distance between them. 'You don't have to do rounds on the weekend. Only if they call you.'

He shrugged. 'Patients are still there. I'll do a round every day unless I can't.' He gestured to the corner of the room. 'You should go back to bed. I think you'll sleep better now.' Then he walked to the door, opened it and quietly closed it after himself. She heard the lock click.

Sam walked away but his thoughts remained focussed on the little cabin on top of the hill. There was something about Ellie, and this place, that connected so strongly with his emotions. He didn't know what it was about her that made him feel so anxious to help. Shame he hadn't been able to break through the barriers to Bree the way he seemed to be able to with Ellie, especially as for the last few years he hadn't really connected to anyone. He glanced out over the bay as he walked down the hill to the hospital. The lighthouse seemed to look down on him with benevolence.

CHAPTER SIX

ELLIE WENT BACK to the bed. Climbed into the clean sheets that a man she'd only known for less than a week had changed for her. She saw the hospital corners and wondered who'd taught him to make a bed like that. It certainly wouldn't have been med school. She looked at the half-full glass of water he'd left her in a fresh glass.

Then she thought of the fact she'd been in her underwear when she'd woken properly, and wondered with pink cheeks when he'd undressed her. Had she helped him, or fought him, or been a limp lump he'd had to struggle with? Had she missed the opportunity of a lifetime?

She frowned at the random and totally inappropriate thought. How on earth would she face him? Then stopped herself. *It's done. You're not eight years old now.*

She considered the result of holding in the swimming pool incident for all those years and even now the tragedy was fading. When Sam returned to Brisbane she'd be able to thank him for that, too.

Her eyes closed and it didn't happen immediately but eventually she drifted off and, strangely, she didn't dream at all.

The next morning was Saturday. Ellie woke after the sun was well and truly up and lay with her eyes open for several minutes as she went over the recent events, both hazy and clear, and how a man who was almost a stranger had taken control of her world, if only for a few hours.

Even a few days ago the idea of that happening would have been ludicrous but in the cold light of day she could be grateful if a little wary. He'd been circumspect, really. Except for taking off her uniform but then she would have done the same if she'd been nursing some-one in the throes of sweaty delirium. She tried not to think of stripping off Sam's shirt and trousers if he was sick—but the option to expand her imagination was tantalising her. *No!*

She glanced at the clock. Almost ten. He said he'd drop in after his weekend round.

When she put her feet on the ground her head didn't hurt. The headache had gone. It had disabled her but now her step was steady as she made her way into the bathroom with an armful of clothes.

By the time she came out, hair piled into a towel, teeth cleaned and mouth washed, she was starting to feel the emptiness in her belly and a hankering for fresh air.

As she opened the door to let the world in, Sam was standing outside with his phone in his hand.

That would be Sam who had seen her frogs and all.

Sam who looked ridiculously handsome. Sam who'd carried her into her bed. 'Oh. Hello. Have you been here long?'

'Just a few minutes. I knocked and when you didn't answer I was going to ring you.'

She opened her eyes wide. 'Do you have my number?'

'The relief midwife gave it to me when I said I might check on you again.'

Confidentiality clauses and all that obviously didn't hold much water when it was Sam asking. Nice of her, she thought sourly. But sensible too. 'I'm much better, thank you.'

She examined him in the bright morning light. Tall. Smiling like he was glad to see her. She shied away from that thought. Not too many shadows under his eyes, considering his onerous midnight duties. 'How are you after spending the evening with a raving woman?'

'Starving.' He gestured to the plastic shopping bag that hung from his hand. 'Any chance of a table and chairs where I can lay this out?'

'Food?' Her stomach grumbled and heat ran up her cheeks. She peeked at him from under her eyelashes to see if he'd heard and saw he was biting his lip. She could see the dimple at the side where he was holding it in.

He'd heard her stomach. Not much mystery left about her for this guy. 'Okay. I'm hungry. So in that case you are very welcome.' Although as she said it she remembered she hadn't made her bed yet, then mentally shrugged.

He'd changed the blinking sheets. He'd survive an

unmade bed. 'We'll take it through to the front deck. We can open the doors from the inside.'

Sam followed her and she was very conscious that the collar on her long-sleeved top wasn't as high as normal and there was some cleavage showing. Maybe she should put on a scarf? Again she reminded herself that he'd seen her in her bra and pants so any more than that was not a concern.

She sighed. He had the advantage of more knowledge of her than she had of him and she didn't like it. In fact she wasn't sure how she'd ended up with a guy who knew so much stuff about her and was walking around in her house like he owned it.

Before he followed her out onto the little veranda, he paused. 'Can I put my milk and cold things in your fridge? I came straight here from the supermarket, but have a few supplies for my flat as well.'

'Sure. There's plenty of room in the fridge.' Ellie winced a little at the hollow emptiness of the food supplies in her kitchen. She needed to shop and restock the cupboards herself.

When he'd done that he followed her to the balcony that overlooked the ocean. She noticed he hesitated at the door.

As he stood there he said quietly, 'Who built these cottages? The view is incredible.'

She stopped and looked in the direction he was looking, sweeping her gaze over the little cliff top that held the three tiny homes, the expanse of the sea out in front of them with the wheeling gulls and fluffy white clouds, the majesty of the tall, white lighthouse on the opposite ridge, which drew visitors on Sundays for lighthouse tours, its tiny top deck enclosed by a white handrail for the visitors as they examined the internal workings of the light through the windows.

'The cottages were built for three spinster sisters in the middle of the last century. They were all nurses at the hospital down the hill.'

She laughed. 'Myra said that the three of us who live here now are modern day reincarnations. Their father ran the lighthouse and when they were in their mid-twenties the eldest came into some money and had the cottages built. There's only one of them alive now. I visit her sometimes in the nursing home. She's ninety and sharp as a tack. Just frail and happy to have other people make her meals now.'

'So they lived here, unmarried, until they were too old and then they moved out?'

'Yep. Fabulous, isn't it?' There were privacy hedges between the three dwellings. In the past the sisters had kept the hedge levels down below waist height but since she'd moved in they'd grown and it was their own little private promontory over the ocean. She loved it. She moved to the edge and peered out at a ship that was far away on the horizon.

When she turned back she could see that Sam was looking uncomfortable and she glanced around to see why. 'You okay?'

'Not a fan of being at the edge of heights.'

'Oh.' The last thing she'd do was make someone with a phobia uncomfortable. 'We'll go back inside, then.'

'No. Just sit me on this side of the table and I'll be

fine.' He lifted the bags up and placed them on the little outdoor table. 'It's perfect here.'

She smiled at him. 'As we dwell in Phobia Central.'

For some silly reason she felt closer to him because he'd admitted to having a weakness for heights. It made her feel not so stupid with her phobia of frogs. She had a sudden horrid thought that perhaps he'd made that up, just to get into her good graces, and then pushed the thought away.

Wayne had done that.

But Sam was not like Wayne. She pushed harder on the thought and it bobbed around in her mind like a cork in a bathtub. She couldn't make it stay down. Sam was not like Wayne, she repeated to herself. Sam told the truth. She hoped.

As if he could read her thoughts, Sam said, 'My aversion to heights is not quite a phobia but I might not be particularly keen to fix the aerial on the roof.'

Somehow, that helped. 'And I'll never be a plumber because of the frogs. You're a good doctor. That's enough.'

'I'm a doctor but not your doctor.' He grinned at her. 'That said, I'm pretty impressed with your recovery mechanism.'

She shrugged. 'I don't get many migraines but when I do get one it's bad.' She didn't add that they usually came after she had the nightmare, or had forced contact with Wayne, and that she'd had fewer nightmares and migraines since she'd shaken him off her trail.

'I can see they wipe you out. If it happens again, you could call me.'

Yeah, right. 'All the way from Brisbane?' She raised her brows at him. At least she knew he was joking. 'Good to know.'

She began laying out the fresh rolls and ham as she reminded herself he'd be gone in a few weeks. Maybe she could just enjoy his company while she had it. It was the first time she'd had a man in her house to share lunch since she'd moved in. Not that she could take any credit for him being here. The only reason it had happened was because he'd invited himself.

It was strange but pleasant. Mostly because she knew it was just a window of opportunity that would close soon when he went back to where he'd come from. Back to his busy trendy life with its 'double shot espresso and milk on the side' lifestyle.

Sam paused as if to say something but didn't. Instead he opened a tray of strawberries and blueberries and produced a tub of Greek yoghurt. 'I'll grab the plates and spoons.' He headed back inside and Ellie looked after him.

'I guess you know where they are,' she murmured more to herself. Then she lifted her voice. 'And grab the butter out of the fridge, please.'

This was all very domestic. Apparently there was nothing like being undressed when semi-delirious for breaking down barriers. But what was she supposed to say? *No. That's my kitchen! Stay out!*

Sam was back while she was still staring after him and mulling over the phenomenon of his intrusion into her world.

He looked so at ease. 'You're very domesticated. Why aren't you married?'

His face stilled. 'My wife died four years ago. It's unlikely I'll marry again.' Then he looked down at the food in his hands.

Oh, heck. 'I'm sorry.' Then added almost to herself, 'Don't you hate that?' The last words fell out as if she hadn't already put her foot in her mouth enough.

He looked up. 'Hate what? When wives die?' He was looking at her quizzically, when really she deserved disapproval. But underneath the lightness of tone was another wall. She could see it as plain as the sun on the ocean below. She knew about walls.

She'd done it again. Talk about lacking tact. She'd said what she thought without thinking. She wasn't usually so socially inept but there was something about this fledgling relationship… She paused at that thought and shied away, slightly horrified.

Anyway… 'I'm making it worse. Of course it's terrible your wife died, but I meant when you ask a question and the worst possible scenario comes back at you and you wished you'd never opened your mouth.'

'I know what you mean. Forget it. A *Monty Python* moment.'

His eyes were shadowed and she hesitated. His wife must have been young. She couldn't help herself.

'How did your wife die?'

He looked up, studied her and then glanced away. 'I'll tell you some time.' Then without looking at her, 'Why do people ask that?'

Now she felt even more inept. Crass. He had answered her and deserved an answer himself. 'I don't know. Curiosity. Because they're afraid of their own mortality?'

That made him look up. 'Are you afraid of your own mortality?'

She shrugged. 'That's a heavy question for eleven in the morning.'

'Heavy question any time of the day,' he said quietly.

The silence lay thick between them. He straightened and looked like he'd wait all day until she answered.

So she did. 'No. I'm not afraid to die. I'm not that special that the world will weep when I'm gone.'

A flash of what looked like pain crossed his face. 'Don't say that. Don't ever say that. Everyone is special and the world will always weep when someone leaves it.'

A breeze tickled her neck from the ocean and she shivered. This conversation was the pits. 'Can we just talk about the weather?'

He stopped. He looked at her and then slowly he smiled, mocking them both. 'Sure. There's a very nice ocean breeze sitting out here.'

She smiled at him primly. Relief rolled over her like one of those swells away down below running in towards the cliffs. A hump. They'd managed to get over a hump. One that she'd caused. 'I like the way the clouds make shadow patterns on the ocean.'

He glanced at the blue expanse a long way below, then away. 'Yes, very nice.'

She looked at the food spread out. Okay. Now it was awkward. 'Eat.'

So they ate. Conversation was minimal and that kept them away from such topics as death and dying, which was fine by Ellie, and gradually their rapport returned and desultory conversation became easy again.

Sam said, 'Josie went home.'

She looked up. 'Did you do the new-born check?'

'Of course.' A pained look. 'Very efficiently.'

That made her smile. 'I have no doubt.' She took a bite of her roll and chewed thoughtfully. She swallowed, then said, 'When you return to your real world in your hospital will you make sure all of your registrars are proficient at checking new-born babies prior to discharge?'

He shrugged. 'There's a little less time for leisurely learning than there is here but I will be asking the question.' He pretended to growl, 'And they'd better be able to answer it.'

Which made her remember that he was a very distinguished and learned man, one many people looked up to, and she was eating rolls with him and treating him like a barely tolerated servant. *Oops.*

She put her roll down. 'Speaking of questions I've been meaning to ask… Do you know anything about midwifery-led birthing units? Do you think it would work here?'

He paused eating his own meal. 'I don't know. Work how?'

She shrugged, looking around for inspiration, how to explain her dream. 'It would be wonderful if we could provide a publicly funded service for pregnant women that didn't need locums.'

'Gee, thanks.' He pretended to be offended.

'Nothing personal. But cover isn't consistent.' She grinned at him. 'I'd like to see a proper centre for planned low-risk births here without having to rely on locum doctors to ensure we can have babies here.' She was gabbling. But she half-expected him to mock her and tell her she was dreaming, that big centres were more financially viable—although she already knew that. But he didn't mock her. She should have had more faith.

'There are models like that springing up all over New South Wales and Victoria.' He said it slowly, as if he was searching around in his mind for what he knew. Ellie could feel herself relax. He wasn't going to tell her she was mad.

He went on. 'Not so many in Queensland yet, but I'm hearing that mothers and midwives are keen. But you'd need more staff.' He gestured to the isolation around them. 'You're a bit of a one-man band here.'

She'd get help. She'd already had two nibbles from the weekend midwives to work here permanently. And why not? A fulfilling job right on the ocean and the chance to become a respected part of a smaller community wasn't to be sniffed at. Trina and Faith were also in.

'We may be a small band at the moment. Or possibly five women, anyway—Trina, Faith, and I and the weekend midwives from the base. If we changed our model of care we could attract more midwives. We would certainly attract more women to birth here if we offered caseload. Most women would love to have the option to have their own midwife throughout the whole pregnancy and birth. Then get followed by them for the next six weeks after the baby is born. It's a wonderful service.'

He studied her for a moment as if weighing up what he was going to say. 'It would be a great service.'

She sagged with relief.

Then he went on, 'Though it does sound demanding for the midwives, seeing as babies come when they want and pregnant women have issues on and off for most of the forty weeks. If one person was responsible for all that—and I imagine you'd have a caseload of about twenty women a year—it seems a huge commitment and would almost certainly affect your private life. Are you prepared for that?'

Private life? What private life. She was a Monday-to-Friday, love-my-job romantic. Not the other sort. But she didn't say any of that.

Instead she said, 'We are. And, paperwork wise, I have a friend who has just set up a service like that on the south coast. She said she'd come up and help me in the early stages. And Myra was a legal secretary before she bought her restaurant. She said she'd give me one day a week.'

'So you have gone into it a bit.' He nodded. Paused. 'And how are you going to deal with emergencies?'

'The same way we deal with them now—stabilise and transfer if needed. But the women will be healthy and the care will be excellent.'

'I have no doubt about that,' he said, and the genuine smile that accompanied the statement warmed her with his faith when he barely knew her.

This wasn't about her as a woman. This was about her as a midwife and she could take compliments about that. 'It's women's choice to decide how and where they want to meet their baby, and women here have been asking for that choice.'

It was so satisfying to have this conversation with somebody who at least understood the questions and the reasons behind them. So she didn't expect the turn when it came.

'Very ideological. So you're going to submerge yourself even deeper in these new families—be available for more times when you're needed—because in my experience babies tend to come in waves. Slow and then all at once. You'll be working sixty hours a week. Be the auntie to hundreds of new babies over the next thirty years.'

'What was he getting at?'

Her smile faltered. 'I hope so.'

His brows were up. She didn't like the expression on his face.

'And wake up at sixty and say "Where has my life gone?"?'

'No.' She shook her head vehemently. 'I'll wake up at sixty and feel like I'm having a life that enriches others.'

The mood plunged with her disappointment. She'd thought he'd seen the vision but now he was looking at her like she needed psychiatric help. Like Wayne used to look at her. That was sad and it was stupid of her to have thought he would be different.

Ooh... Ellie could feel the rage build. Somewhere inside she knew it was out of proportion to what he'd said. That if she chose that path it didn't mean she'd never have a family of her own. But him saying that seemed to ignite her anger.

She leaned towards him. 'How is that different from your life? You said yourself you're probably not going to marry again or have children. Will you spend the next thirty years working? How is that different to me?'

He shrugged. 'I'm a man. It's my job to work till I'm sixty-five or seventy, so it should be rewarding.'

'You're a chauvinist. My working life deserves re-ward too. How about you stay barefoot and pregnant and make my dinner while I go to work? Is that okay?'

Sam had no idea how the conversation had become so heated. One minute it had been warm and friendly—she'd been gradually relaxing with him—and then she'd waxed on about giving the rest of her life to strangers like some first world saint and he'd found himself get-ting angry.

He needed to remind himself that he was a man who respected women's choices, and of course he respected her choice. She was right. He should recognise that what she wanted to do was parallel to his own ambition of single-minded dedication. And look how useless that had been for getting over Bree's death. Maybe it was because he did recognise himself in what she said that he'd reacted so stupidly to seeing it through her eyes.

He took one look at her face and concluded he needed to redeem himself fast or he'd be out on his ear with his blueberries in his lap.

He held up both hands in surrender. 'I'm sorry. I

have no right to judge your life decisions. You should choose your path and do whatever fulfils you. Truce.'

Her open mouth shut with a click and he knew he'd just averted Armageddon. Wow.

She was a feisty little thing when she didn't like what he said. And, come to think of it, what the heck had come over him? If she wanted to grow old in this eyrie of a house, alone every night just living for her work, then that was her choice. A small voice asked if that wasn't his choice too. He might not live on top of a cliff, but it wasn't so different from his trendy city flat overlooking the Brisbane River that he barely saw and the twenty-four-seven availability he gave his own hospital.

He'd known her for less than a week and already he was sticking his nose in. Normally he didn't even see other people and what they were doing with their lives but the idea of Ellie's future life made him go cold. It sounded very like his and he wanted more for her. He shivered.

She sat stonily staring out over the ocean and he could discern the slow breaths she was taking to calm down. Typical midwife—deep breathing experts. His mouth twitched and he struggled to keep it under control. Imagine if she saw him laughing at her.

They were both being silly. Fighting about the next thirty years when they should be enjoying the present moment. He was here with a gorgeously interesting woman. He wasn't sure when she'd changed from pretty to gorgeous, but the word definitely fit her better. The sun was drying her dark hair, bringing out red highlights, and the ocean stretched away behind her. He liked the way her hair fell heavily on her neck when she didn't have it in the pony tail. He could remember the weighty silkiness of it in his hand as he'd held it off her face as he'd soothed her during her nightmare.

He remembered unbuttoning her shirt when she'd lifted her hand to her buttons as if the neckline and collar were choking her. He'd slipped the whole shirt off her shoulders, and she'd pushed at her buttoned work trousers, so he'd helped with those too. She'd relaxed back into the cool sheets with relief and he'd covered her up, trying to blot out the delectable picture of her golden skin in lacy bra and briefs. Feeling a little apprehensive about what she'd say to him when she woke.

'You.' She turned towards him and his little flight of fantasy crashed and burned. Apparently the deep breathing hadn't worked.

'Tell me how your wife died!' There was nothing warm and fuzzy about the request.

That snapped him out of his rosy fantasies and the guilt he mostly kept at bay from his failure to save Bree swamped him. He didn't know why he answered her.

'She killed herself.'

CHAPTER SEVEN

'It looked like a parachute accident. Except she left a note.' He kept staring at his clenched fingers. Didn't look at her. He couldn't believe he'd said that to a stranger and opened himself up to the inevitable questions.

Ellie's voice was a whisper. 'Oh, heck.' Closer than before. 'Why would she do that?'

He figured he might as well get the rest out. Be done with it. 'Because we lost our third baby at twenty weeks' gestation and she said she couldn't go on.' His voice was flat because if he let the emotion in it would demolish him. His inability to help his own family had destroyed Bree. 'I was next to useless, and using work to bury my own grief, and she refused to talk about it together. We drifted apart. Each suffering in our own way but unable to connect. Then it was too late.'

Her voice was different now. Compassionate. 'Is that why you were so determined Marni be transferred?'

He jerked back to the present with the question. Her thought processes were way different to his. He took a deep breath of his own. Was that the only satisfaction he'd had in the last four years?

Sam thought about what she'd asked. It had kept him sane, having a mission. 'Probably. Since Bree died I've been working on a regime for women who have repeat extreme premature labours, and the results have been promising with the new treatments.'

When he looked up from his hands he saw she was beside him. Her voice was soft. 'Your way of managing the grief?'

'Or the guilt.' Why was he talking about this? He never spoke about Bree. Her hand touched his shoulder as she bent over him. It was feather-light but he felt the pressure as if it was burning into him like a hot coal through ice. Melting him.

'What was she like? What did she do? Your dad must have been upset as well.'

'Before the babies Bree was happy. A great paediatrician, wonderful with kids. Afterwards...' he paused and shook his head, speaking so quietly it was as if he'd forgotten she was there. 'She hid her depression using work too. We both did. She said she wanted more space. When she died my dad felt almost as bad as I did that we hadn't seen it coming. So it was tough for him as well.'

She leant her head down and put her face against his hair. 'I'm sorry for your loss.' Her lemony freshness surrounded him like angel dust as she reached down and hugged him.

Nobody had hugged him since Bree had died. His dad was more of handshake kind of guy and he didn't have any women friends. Then she slid her hands around his shoulders, pulled his head onto her chest and stroked his hair. Her hands were warm whispers of comfort, infused with empathy. 'I'm so sorry. But it's not your fault.'

He twisted his head and looked at her, saying very slowly and deliberately, his voice harsh and thick, 'You've got as much right to say that as I had to say you can't waste your life the way you're planning to.'

He thought she'd draw away at that. He hoped she would because the scent was fogging his brain and the emotions of the last few minutes were far too volatile for bodily contact. All those fantasies he'd been battling with since he'd arrived in this damn place were rising like mist off the ocean. She was holding him close. Pulling him in like a siren on a rock. Drowning him.

She pressed her face against his. 'I should never have asked. We're both too nosy.' She kissed his cheek as if she couldn't help herself. 'I'm sorry.'

If he'd thought her enticing while he watched her from a distance, up close she was irresistible. The scent of her, the feel of her, the warmth of her, was intoxicating, and when she leaned in to say something else he lifted his mouth and captured hers as it passed. She stilled—she tasted like the first day of spring.

She'd made it happen. The kiss had been an apology. A dangerous one. Kissing Sam was a mistake because when he kissed her back driving him away was the last thing on her mind.

Somehow she was on his lap, both her arms were around his hard shoulders, and he was holding her mouth against him with a firm palm to the back of her head.

Inhaling his scent, his taste, his maleness was glorious. The kiss seemed to go on and on even though it was only a minute. His mouth was a whole subterranean world of wonder. In heated waves he kissed her and she kissed him back in time to the crash of the ocean below—rising and falling, sometimes peaking in a crest and then drawing Ellie down into a swirling world she was lost in…one she hadn't visited before. Until the phone rang.

It took a few moments for the sound to penetrate and then she felt his hand ease back.

He pulled away but his eyes were dark and hot as he watched her blink. She raised her trembling fingers to her lips.

His voice was deep, too damn sexy, and he smiled at her in a way that made her blush. 'Your phone is ringing.'

She blinked. Scrambled off his lap. 'Right.' She blinked again and then bolted for the phone while all the time her mind was screaming, *what the heck made you start that?*

It was the weekend midwife, Roz. 'Can you come, Ellie? One of the holidaymakers from the caravan park is in labour. Just walked in. Thirty-five weeks. Twins. Feeling pushy. I'll ring the doctor next.'

'Twins! Sam's here. I'll bring him. We'll be there in three minutes. Get help from the hospital to make some calls. Get them to ring the ambulance to come ASAP.'

Ellie strode to the door where Sam was collecting dishes away from the edge from his side of the table. 'Let's go, Sam. Thirty-five-week twins. Second stage.'

Ellie was pulling on her sneakers. She could put a surgical gown over her clothes.

Sam matched Ellie's calm professional face. 'My car's outside.'

They were there in less than two minutes. Just before they arrived, Sam said, 'Ellie?'

She looked at him. She was still off-balance but immensely glad her mind could be on a hundred things other than what position she'd been in and where that could have led only five minutes ago.

This was an emergency. She'd had two sets of twins when she'd been working with a midwife in the centre of Australia. She'd need to watch out for so many things in the coming hour. They had very little equipment for prems. They'd either have a birth of two premature babies here or a harrowing trip to the base hospital. Twin births could be tricky.

'Ellie?'

'What?'

Sam's voice was so calm. 'This is what I do. Thirty-five-week twins are fine. Not like pre-viable twins. Everything will be fine.'

Ellie felt the tension ease to a more useful alertness. He was asking for a little faith in the team. She smiled at him. 'Okay. You're right.'

A dusty campervan with flowers and a slogan painted on it sat haphazardly in the car park. There was no sign of anyone as they hurried through the doors to the maternity unit but sounds coming from the birthing rooms indicated action.

'We'll just use the one neo-natal resuscitation trolley. The other's too slow to heat up and warmth will be the issue.' Ellie was thinking of the babies. The twins could stay together if they needed help. They'd been closer than that inside their mum and might even comfort each other if kept together.

The obstetric part, Sam could handle. Thank goodness. The mother might not feel lucky at the moment but she was.

They entered the room one after the other and the relief on Roz's face would have been comical if the situation hadn't been so serious. 'Her waters just broke. Nine centimetres. At least it's clear and not meconium-stained.'

Then Roz collected herself. Glancing apologetically at the mother and father, she explained, 'Dr Southwell's an obstetrician from Brisbane Mothers and Babies, and this is the midwife in charge here, Ellie. This is Annette and Paul Keen.'

Everyone tried hard to smile at each other. Sam succeeded and Ellie gave them a wave on her way to sort out the required equipment in case they needed to resuscitate either baby or, heaven forbid, both.

Roz was reciting, 'Annette's twins were due in five weeks. They were packing up from the park to go home today. Labour started an hour ago but she thought she had a tummy bug because Paul had one a few days ago.'

Annette opened her mouth to say hello and changed it to a groan as the next wave of contraction hit her. She ground out, 'I feel like pushing.'

Sam stepped closer to the bed. He looked into the terrified woman's face as she sat high in the bed with

lines of strain creasing her face and touched her arm.
'I'm Sam. It's okay, Annette, we've got this. You just
listen to your body and your babies, let go of the fear
and we'll do the rest. It's their birthday.'

Ellie's hands paused on the suction as she heard his
voice and in that moment realised what she was missing in her life. A safe harbour. It would never be Sam,
but just maybe someone somewhere might be out there
for her, someone like this man who could invest so
much comfort in words and took the time to offer them.
Such a man would be worth coming home to. She wondered if he had always been such a calming influence.
Whether he'd grown to understand a parent's fears since
his own loss.

'It's my fault,' Paul mumbled from the corner of
the room as he twisted his hands. 'I should never have
pushed for this holiday before the babies were born. It's
my fault.' Ellie glanced his way but it looked like nobody else had heard him.

Roz bent down and placed the little Doppler on
Annette's stomach. First one and then, after she shifted
to the other side of Annette's magnificent belly, another
heartbeat echoed around the room.

Sam nodded, patted Annette's arm, turned, walked
to the sink and washed his hands.

Ellie checked the oxygen and air cylinders were full
and then moved to Paul's side. She spoke very quietly
so no one else could hear. 'You heard the doctor, Paul.
The time for worrying is gone. Now is the time to be
the rock Annette needs you to be. Hold her hand. Share
the moment. You're about to be a father.'

Paul's eyes locked on hers and he nodded jerkily. 'Right. Rock.' He looked at his hand and scurried over to his wife. He took up her fingers and kissed them. 'Sorry. Lost it for a minute.'

Annette squeezed his hand and Ellie saw the man's fingers go white. Saw Paul wince as the pressure increased and with a smile her eyes were drawn to Sam as he stood quietly at the side of the bed with his gloved fingers intertwined, waiting. As if they had all the time in the world and this was a normal day. She felt the calm settle in the room and smiled quietly to herself.

Roz folded back the sheets to above Annette's thighs.

The first twin came quickly, a fine scattering of hair on her head, a thick coating of white vernix covering her back, and then she slipped into Sam's waiting hands. Not as small as they'd feared, probably over two thousand, five hundred grams, which was good for a twin.

The little girl feebly protested at the brush of air on her skin until Ellie wiped her quickly with a towel and settled her against her mother with a warmed bunny rug over her back. Annette's hands came down to greet her as she shifted the sticky little body so she could see her. The mother's face was round with wonder.

'Oh, my. Hello, little Rosebud.'

Ellie smiled to herself at the name, actually appropriate for the pink pursed mouth, and positioned the tiny girl strategically to make room for the next baby, making sure her chin was angled to breathe easily.

Ellie slipped a pink knitted beanie on the downy head. The soft cap was too big but would do the job of keeping her little head warm and slow the loss of heat.

When she glanced at Paul, tears were sliding down his cheeks as he gazed in awe at his wife and new daughter.

Annette's brows drew together but this time she was confident. 'I need to push again.'

Paul started, and Ellie grabbed another towel and blanket from the stack Roz had collected under the warmer. They all waited.

'This one's breech,' Sam said quietly.

The contraction passed and they all waited for the next.

Annette breathed out heavily and Ellie looked down and saw the little bottom and scrotum inching out, the cord falling down as the belly and back eased up in a long sweep. First one leg sprang free and then, finally, the other leg. It was happening so fast. The contraction finished and they all waited.

'Going beautifully,' Sam murmured two minutes later as the pale shoulders rotated and birthed one by one, followed by the arms, in a slow dance of angles and rotations that magically happened the way nature intended thanks to the curves of his mother's pelvis.

Ellie stood awed at how quickly the baby was delivering by himself.

Sam hadn't touched the torso. His gloved fingers hovered just above in case baby took a wrong turn as it went through the normal mechanisms and she remembered the mantra 'hands off the breech'. He was certainly doing that.

Then, unexpectedly, the rapid progress stopped. Annette pushed again. Just the head to come, Ellie thought. *Come on.* Annette was still pushing.

'Deflexed head,' Sam muttered and glanced at Ellie. He slipped his arm under the baby's body to support it and gently felt for the face with his lower hand. With the hand she could see he placed his second and fourth fingers on each side of the baby's nape at the back.

'Annette. We need to flex the baby's head for birth. I'm going to get Ellie to push on your tummy just above the pelvic bone.'

Annette hissed an assent as she concentrated.

Sam went on. 'Ellie, palpate just above the pelvic brim. You'll feel the head. Lean on that ball firmly while I tip baby's chin down from here.' He glanced at Annette. 'Don't be surprised if baby needs to go to the resus trolley for a bit to wake up, okay?'

Paul's eyes widened. Annette nodded as she concentrated. Ellie could feel the solid trust in the room and marvelled how Sam had achieved that in so short a time. It was worth its weight in gold when full co-operation was needed.

Sam's firm voice. 'Okay, push, Annette. Lean, Ellie.'

Ellie did as she was asked and suddenly the head released. Baby's chin must have shifted towards his chest, allowing the smaller diameters of the head under the pubic arch and through the pelvis, and in a steady progression the whole head was born. Sam expelled a breath and Ellie began to breathe again too.

The little boy was limp in Sam's hands.

Paul swayed and Roz pushed the chair under him. 'Sit.' The dad collapsed back into the chair with his hand over his mouth.

Sam quickly clamped and cut the cord and Ellie

reached in, wiped the new-born with the warm towel and bundled him up to transfer to the resuscitation trolley. 'Come over when you're up to it, Paul,' she said over her shoulder as she went.

Sam spoke to Roz. 'Can you take over here, Roz? Call out if you need me.' He followed Ellie.

Ellie hit the timer on to measure how long since birth, and dried the new-born with another warm towel to stimulate him, but he remained limp.

Sam positioned the baby's head in a sniffing position and applied the tiny mask over his chin and nose. The little chest rose and fell with Sam's inflation of the lungs through the mask.

Ellie listened to the baby's chest. 'Heart rate eighty.' She applied the little pulse oximeter to the baby's wrist which would allow them to see how much oxygen from their lung inflations was circulating in the baby's body.

'Thirty seconds since birth,' Ellie said, and leant down to listen to his heart rate again, even though the oximeter had picked it up now. 'Seventy.' If the rate fell below sixty they would have to do cardiac massage.

'Okay,' Sam said and continued watching the steady rise and fall of the small chest. They both knew it wasn't great but it also wasn't dire yet. Babies were designed to breathe. Unlike adults, new-born babies needed inflation of their lungs to start, were respiratory driven, and even more important than cardiac massage was the initiation of breathing and the expulsion of the fluid from the untried lungs.

Ellie reminded herself she had great faith in the way

babies had recovered from much more dramatic births than this one.

Sam continued with his inflations for another thirty seconds, Ellie wrote down the observations and finally the baby wriggled a tiny bit. Ellie felt the tension ease. 'Come on, junior.'

'His name is Thorn.' Paul was there and he wasn't swaying. He seemed to have pulled himself together. 'Come on, Thorn,' he said sternly, staring down at his son. 'This is your dad speaking. Wake up.'

Ellie decided it was just coincidence but Thorn's blue eyes opened at the command. The baby blinked and struggled and began to cry. The pulse oximeter rate flew from eighty to a hundred and thirty in the blink of an eye and Sam eased back on the mask.

'Well, that worked,' she said and smiled at Paul. A sudden exuberance was bubbling inside her and she looked across at Sam, who grinned back at her. She guessed he was feeling it too.

'Good work, Thorn,' Roz's relieved voice called across and Ellie heard Annette's shaky relief as she laughed.

Thorn was roaring now and, after a glance at Sam and catching his nod, Ellie scooped the baby up and carried him back to his mother. He was soon nestled in beside his sister on his mother's chest.

There was a knock on the door and one of the young ambulance officers poked her head in. 'Did you guys call us?'

Sam said, 'Thanks for coming. Transfer to the base hospital, thirty-five-week twins, but we'd like to wait half an hour—check the bleeding is settled and babies stable—if you want to come back.'

'We'll have coffee. Haven't had lunch. Ring us when you're ready.' She looked to the bed. 'Congratulations.' Then she disappeared.

Ellie decided that was eminently sensible. The impact of an urgent emergency transfer of all concerned would have ruined the moment when everyone was settled. More brownie points for Sam.

She wouldn't have taken the responsibility for delaying transfer but having an obstetrician on site made all the difference. It was fabulous for Annette and Paul to have a chance to collect themselves before they had to leave.

Roz was standing beside Annette, helping her sort the babies, and Sam and Ellie went over to the sink to strip off their gloves and apply new ones.

'Rosebud and Thorn,' Sam said in an undertone, and his eyes were alight with humour.

The names clicked. 'Cute,' she whispered back, grinning, and realised this was a moment she wasn't used to—savouring the feeling of camaraderie and a sudden urge to throw her arms around Sam and dance a little.

She whispered, 'That was very exciting and dramatic. Thank goodness everything is great.'

'Ditto.' Sam grinned at her.

Normally the nurse from the hospital disappeared as soon as the birth was safely complete, and most of the locums were burnt out and uninterested, so as soon as the excitement was over Ellie didn't usually have a third person to talk over the birth with. 'I'll remember that hint with the after-coming head if I have another un-expected breech delivery,' she said now, thinking back over Thorn's birth. The two breeches she'd been present at before had progressed to birth easily.

Sam nodded sagely. 'He was star-gazing. Silly boy. You have to keep your chin tucked in if you want your head to pop out.'

Ellie bit her lip to stop the laugh. Stargazing… A funny way to say it, but clear as a bell to her. She smiled up at him as the last of the tension inside her released.

She stayed with Roz in birthing until the ambulance officers returned. Thorn and Rosebud were positioned twin style at each breast and did an excellent job with their first breastfeeding lesson in life. Besotted parents marvelled, wept and kept thanking the three staff, so much so that Sam escaped from the room to write up the transfer papers.

Just under an hour after the twins were born, Ellie and Sam stood watching as they were loaded into the back of the ambulance.

'Come back and visit us next year when you come on your holiday. We'd love to see you all.' Ellie said.

She'd offered to go in the ambulance but Roz had laughed and said she should take the easy job and stay with the empty ward. Hopefully nobody would come in. Surely they'd had their quota for the week?

Which left Ellie and Sam standing at the door, waving off the ambulance.

As the vehicle turned out of the driveway Ellie told herself to keep her mind on what needed to be done but she could feel Sam's gaze. She kept her own on the spot where the ambulance disappeared and then suddenly turned away. Over her shoulder she said, 'Thank you. You were great. I'll be fine now.'

Sam didn't move. 'So I should go?' His voice was quiet, neutral, so she had to stop or it would have been rude. But her feet itched to scoot away as fast as she could because this man was the one she had kissed. On whose lap she had squirmed and wanted more. *Oh, my*—where was she supposed to look?

She didn't decide on flight quickly enough.

Still quietly, he said, 'You don't need me any more—that right? And we both pretend this morning didn't happen? Is that what you want, Ellie?' She didn't say anything so he added, 'Just checking.' There was definite sardonic tinge to that last statement.

She forced herself to look at him. Maybe she could tell him the truth about Wayne. Because she wasn't going to pursue any crumbs of attention he wanted to give her for the next three weeks and it was all her fault this morning had got out of hand. Maybe she owed him that—telling him how she'd been made a fool of. Lied to. Ridiculed. Abused. She shuddered at the thought. Or perhaps she owed him an apology. She could do that at least.

'I'm sorry, Sam. I don't know what happened. It's all my fault, and I apologise. Can't we just blame the aftermath of my migraine for the strange behaviour on my part and forget it?'

He was studying her thoughtfully, and for so long that Ellie felt like an insect under a magnifying glass.

Finally he said, 'What if I don't want to forget it? What if I want to hear the rest of your stories?'

Why would he want to do that? She couldn't do that. Should never have started it. 'You'll have to do without. Because there'll be no repeat.' She heard the finality in her voice and hoped he did too. 'I'd like you to go now, please.'

Sam looked at the woman in front of him and felt the frustration of the impenetrable wall between them yet again. The really disturbing thing was an inexplicable certainty that Ellie Swift wasn't supposed to be like this. It made no sense. He could very clearly see that underneath the prickly exterior and gazetted loner lay a warm and passionate woman he wanted to know more about. Wanted to lose himself in kissing again. And more.

That she'd had a disastrous relationship was of course the most likely reason she was like this. Underneath her armour lay something or someone who had scarred her and she wasn't risking that kind of pain again. He got that. Boy, did he get that. But it wasn't all about the frog phobia. There had to be something else.

But whether or not he'd get the opportunity to explore that conundrum and the tantalising glimpses of the woman who had reached down and kissed him with such sweetness was a very moot point.

Maybe he should just cut and run. Do what he always did when he felt things were getting too personal or emotional. But, for the first time since Bree had died, he wanted to explore the way he was feeling. Wanted to find out if this glimpse he'd had of a better life was real, or if he was just suffering from some unexpected aberration he'd forget about when he went back to the real world.

Maybe he'd better research his own reasons for pursuing Ellie first before he caused any more damage to this vulnerable woman in front of him, and it was only that overriding consideration which finally made him agree to leave. Since Bree's death he'd lost his confidence in his own emotional stability.

CHAPTER EIGHT

ELLIE WATCHED HIM go and, after having asked him to leave, now, conversely, wanted him to stay. It was the kiss that stopped her asking him to come back. Ellie had never tried to hurt anyone in her life before—so why had she hurt Sam by asking him so baldly about his wife? He was already punishing himself and didn't need her input. He'd been mortally wounded by his love—she knew how that felt—and she'd broken open his unhealed wound with her harsh request. He'd deserved none of it.

So she'd kissed him better—and to make herself feel better. Although 'better' wasn't really the right word for what she'd felt.

Ellie had an epiphany. She'd wanted to hurt him because that way she'd drive him away for her own safety—she'd had no kind thought for him.

And then they'd kissed and everything had changed. And she was running scared. It had all been pushed back by the birth of the twins but the reality was—things had changed.

Ellie sighed. It would have been good to talk more

about the birth. He could have stayed for that. And that was the only reason, she told herself.

She looked around the empty ward, disorientated for a moment. Then she busied herself pushing books across the desk.

It was Sunday tomorrow and she probably needed the space from this man. He was taking up too much room in her head. Luckily she had a whole day to get her head sorted by Monday.

She slowly turned towards the birthing unit and walked in to strip the bed. What a morning. Premature twins. That was a first for her since she'd arrived last year. Thank goodness everything had progressed smoothly.

She thought about Sam's expertise with Thorn's birth in the breech position. Sam's calmness. She wanted to cry, which was stupid. It was Sam's quiet confidence that had made them all seamless in their care and his rock-solid capability that made it so positive and not fraught as it could have been for Paul and Annette with a less experienced practitioner. How lucky they'd been that it had been Sam. She dragged her mind away from where it wanted to go.

She had to stay away from Sam's hands holding her, his lips on hers, their breaths mingled. No. If she let Sam in and he let her down like Wayne had, she suspected she'd never, ever recover.

She took herself into the small staff change room and opened her locker where she kept a spare clean uniform. She'd been stuck here before out of uniform and didn't like it.

She told herself that was the reason she needed more armour. She took off her loose trousers and blouse and pulled on the fitted blue work trousers and her white-collared shirt and buttoned it to the top. Funny how she felt protected by the uniform. Professional and capable. Not an emotional idiot throwing out accusations and making stupid moves on men who were just being kind.

What an emotional roller coaster the last few days had been. And action packed on the ward.

By rights they should have no babies for a week or more because the ward had been too crazy since Sam had arrived. Maybe he drew the excitement to him like a magnet. She grimaced. He certainly did that in more ways than one and she needed to put that demon to sleep.

By the time Roz returned Ellie had the ward returned to its pristine orderliness, and the paper work sorted and filed. Ellie stood up to leave but Roz put her hand on her arm.

Looking a little worse for wear, Roz said, 'Please stay for a bit. Have a cup of tea with me. I'm bursting to talk about it. Not often you get to see twins born without any intervention. Wasn't Dr Sam awesome?' Roz's eyes were shining and she was obviously still on a high from the birth.

Ellie didn't have the heart to leave. She put the plastic bag with her bundled civilian clothes down.

'Sure. Of course. The jug's just boiled. I'll make a pot while you freshen up if you want?'

Roz nodded and Ellie had to smile at the bouncy excitement that exuded from her.

Roz was right. This was an opportunity to think about how they'd handled the situation, what they'd done well and what they could possibly have done better. All future planning for a unit she wanted to see become one of the best of its kind.

She couldn't believe Sam had driven all her normal thought processes into such confusion. *See?* She needed to stay on track and not be diverted by good-looking doctors who had the capacity to derail all her plans.

As Ellie made a pot of tea and brought two cups to the desk she knew with a pang of discomfort that a week ago Roz wouldn't have been able to drag her away from talking about the birth and the outcomes. Maybe it was just that she'd been sick. Maybe it had nothing to do with the fact that she was running scared because a certain man had disturbed her force field and anything to do with talking about him made her want to run a mile.

'I can't get over the breech birth.' Roz was back. Her hair was brushed, lipstick reapplied and she looked as animated as Ellie had ever seen her. She could feel the energy and excitement and welcomed the uncomplicated joy Roz exuded, because joy was dearly bought.

Yes. They should be celebrating. Every midwife loved the unexpected birth that progressed fast and complication-free with a great outcome. And when it was twins it was twice as exciting.

'I just feel so lucky I was here.' Roz's eyes were glowing and Ellie felt the tension slipping away. She was glad Roz asked her to stay.

Roz went on. 'But I was super-glad when you two

walked in together. Especially since, the last time I saw you, you looked like death warmed up.'

Roz stopped and thought about that. 'Did you say on the phone you were together when I called?'

Ellie fought to keep the colour out of her cheeks. 'Dr Southwell had dropped in to ask if I needed anything. But I'm usually good when the migraine goes. It just takes about twelve hours. I'm feeling normal now.' Or as normal as she could, considering the emotional upheavals of the last few days.

Roz studied her. 'You're still a bit pale. And I shouldn't be keeping you here on your day off. Sorry.'

'No. It's good to talk about it. You're right. You did really well getting us here, and everything was ready. You must have got a shock when they walked in and you realised you were actually going to have the babies.'

Roz nodded enthusiastically, totally diverted from the how Ellie and Sam had walked in together. Thank goodness. Ellie returned her attention to Roz, cross with herself, as her brain kept wandering off topic.

'Paul was almost incoherent, Annette was still in the car and I didn't get that it was twins until she was in here and I saw how big she was. Then he said they were premature and she was booked in to have them at the tertiary hospital and I nearly had a heart attack. All I could think about was ringing you, and I was hoping like heck you'd be able to come.'

'I'm fine. But I guess we need to plan that a bit better for the future too. Maybe make a list to work down if one of the call-ins can't make it, rather than ringing around at the time when you have much better things to do than make phone calls.'

Roz nodded agreement. She said thoughtfully, 'I did get the nurse over from the main hospital, and she could have phoned around if needed.'

How it should be. 'That's great. And the babies came out well, which is always a relief.'

Roz frowned as she remembered. 'The boy was a bit stunned. Annette and Paul weren't the only ones worried.'

Ellie thought about Thorn as he'd lain unmoving under their hands, of Sam's presence beside her as they'd worked in unison, both wordlessly supporting the other as they'd efficiently managed the resuscitation. Her stomach clenched as she remembered. At the time it had been all action with no time to be emotionally involved. It was afterwards they thanked their lucky stars everything had worked out well.

That was why debriefing became important, because clearing stark pictures by talking about them and explaining the reasons let her release mental stresses.

Ellie said, 'He wasn't responding for a bit. We gave him an Apgar of three at one minute but by five minutes he was an eight out of ten. I've only been at a few breech births and they often do seem to take a little longer than cephalic births to get going.'

Roz nodded as she thought about it. 'I guess it could be that the cord is out and it has to be compressed against the body coming through. Or the rapid descent of the head afterwards might stun them too. But he came good by two minutes.'

The door opened and they both looked up. Sam was back. Ellie felt her heart give a little leap but it was followed by a frown as all her indecision and tangled emotions flooded back with full force. Damn. She'd been engrossed in this discussion and should have made her escape.

Her face must have shown her displeasure because he raised his brows. 'Sorry for interrupting.'

'No. Come in. Welcome!' Roz jumped up. 'Have a cup of tea with us. It's great you're here.' She turned to Ellie. 'Isn't it, Ellie? We were just talking about the birth.'

Sam looked at her. 'I'll come back.' Then he turned to Roz. 'I thought Ellie had gone and I wondered if you had any questions, Roz. It was a big morning.'

Ellie heard his words and felt ashamed. She reached down inside and retrieved the normal Ellie from the layers of confusion. Found her equilibrium. There she was—the one who'd greeted him, had it been only six days ago?

She smiled almost naturally. 'Please stay. I was going but you're both right. It's really good to talk over things while they are fresh in our minds. We were talking about breech babies that take a while to respond after birth.'

The conversation that followed was all Ellie hoped it would be. Sam shared his fierce intellect and grasp of the intricacies of breech birth from a consultant's perspective—they even covered a spirited discussion on the pros and cons of breech birth for first-time mums—

and by the time she was ready to leave Ellie was comfortable again in Sam's company.

Or perhaps it would be fairer to say in Dr Southwell's company, because she was every inch the woman behind the uniform in charge of the ward and her feet were very firmly planted in the real world of the hospital that she loved.

'I'll leave you two to talk more. I'm going home.'

Sam stood up. 'I'll come with you. I need to grab the milk I left in your fridge.'

They both stood and as Ellie walked to the door with him she heard Roz murmur after them, 'Better than checking out her collection of stamps.' Ellie winced and pretended she didn't hear.

'The breech was great,' Ellie said to change the subject. They went out into the sunlight and Ellie was thankfully aware of the cool ocean breeze brushing her face—helping calm the blush that heated her cheeks.

'So, was it easy to find the hard baby's head through the abdomen when you leant down on it?' Sam asked her with a smile on his face. They had shared something special.

Ellie thought back to the moment when little Thorn's birth progress had stalled. The sudden increase in tension in the room. The mother pushing and nothing happening. The clock ticking. The baby's body turning pale. Then the calm voice of Sam instructing her to help with downward pressure just above the mother's pubic bone.

'Yes. A solid little ball that just pushed away, and then he was born.' She pictured the baby's position in her mind. 'So his chin must have lifted and changed the diameters of the presenting part which made him jam up. It certainly made a difference to re-tuck his chin in, and then he was born. All great learning experiences that make sense when you think about it.'

'Something simple like that can change the outcome so dramatically. The days of pulling down on a breech baby, which of course made the chin obstruct further, thankfully have gone.'

'I've seen two other normal breech births, the rest have been caesareans, so it was a great learning experience for me.'

'You have good instincts. Listen to them and you'll be fine.'

It was a nice thing to say, but she didn't know what to do with the compliment because it was midwifery-orientated but also personal. So she changed the subject. The crashing of the waves from beyond the headland seemed louder than normal. Instead of turning up the hill to her house Ellie turned her head towards the ocean. 'The sea's rough today! I'm up for a walk out to the lighthouse before I go home. If you'd like to have a look, you could come. I need to lose some excess energy.'

'So, excitement makes you energetic?'

She shrugged. 'I'm energetic most of the time.' Except when she had nightmares, but she was well over that now. Luckily they didn't leave her listless for long. 'So what have you been doing on your time off? Have you looked around the bay? Met anybody interesting?'

Sam nodded mock-solemnly. 'My friend with the

ingrown toenail is my new best bud. He dropped off a dozen prawns yesterday at lunchtime and offered me a trip on his trawler but I said I needed to be on call.'

She'd never been interested in offshore fishing but she was happy to hop on board a small tin dinghy and putt-putt around the creek.

'Would you like to go out on a prawn trawler?'

'It'd be interesting. Different way of spending your life than in a hospital seven days a week.'

She threw a look at him. 'Seven days a week is not healthy.'

He raised his brows. His long stride shortened to match her shorter one. 'I thought we'd agreed to disagree on how the other person spends their life.'

Oops. 'That's true. Let's talk about lighthouses. Lighthouse keepers worked seven days a week and only had one holiday a year.'

There was a pause while he digested that. 'Lighthouses. Yes. Let's talk about lighthouses.' The smile he gave her was so sweet she had a sudden vision of Sam as a very young boy with the innate kindness she could see in him now. She couldn't say why, but she knew without a doubt he would never tease a heartbroken little girl who missed her mummy. He would more likely scold anyone who did. She really liked that little boy.

She blinked away the silly fantasy and brought herself back to the hillside path they were on now. The grassy path wound along the edge of the cliff edge, a pristine white fence separated them from the drop and tufts of grass hid the crumbly edge. It was maintained by the present custodian of the lighthouse who lived off site. Glancing at Sam she manoeuvred herself to the side of the path nearest the cliff.

'The lighthouse was built in the eighteen hundreds and is part of a network that was built right along the eastern seaboard after ships were floundering on the underwater rocks.'

He was smiling at something then paused, turned and looked at her.

'Are you listening to me being your guide?'

He grinned. 'Sorry. I was thinking I could see you as a lighthouse keeper.'

She thought about that. Yes, she could have been a lighthouse keeper. 'Except the position was only open to men—though they did prefer married men with families.'

He smiled at that. 'I imagine they would have big families if stuck in a lighthouse together.'

She grinned at him. 'The first couple who lived here had eleven children. He'd been a widower and he fell in love with a local girl—said the bay and the woman he found here healed him. They ended up with a big family. All natural births and all survived.'

'What an amazing woman. And did they live here happily-ever-after?'

'They moved to a lighthouse with bigger family quarters. Once in the lighthouse business, you tended to stay in the lighthouse business.'

'She should have been a midwife.' He laughed at that. 'The children would have had a wonderful childhood.'

'Some families were very isolated but at least here,

at the bay, the children went to school and played with other children.'

They arrived at the top of the hill. The base of the lighthouse and the tall tower were painted pristine white with concrete walls that were a third of a metre thick, which gave a hint at how solid the lighthouse was. They both looked up to the wrought-iron rail away at the top where the windows and the light were.

'They have a tour tomorrow. You can go up the stairs inside and come out onto the walkway. It's a great view.'

Sam patted the solid walls. 'Is this how thick the walls of your cottage are?'

'Yep. It wasn't usual for lighthouses to be built of concrete but there's a couple on the north coast like that. I think the sisters liked it and that's why they copied it.'

Sam watched her glance across the bay in the direction of the three cliff-top dwellings.

She went on. 'I love knowing my cottage is strong. I know the big bad wolf can't blow my house down.'

He'd suspected that was a reason she was holed away here in her house with thick walls. 'Do you want to tell me about your big bad wolf?'

'Nope.' She glanced his way but her eyes skidded past his without meeting them. 'Why spoil the afternoon?'

She pushed past the lighthouse into the little forecourt that looked over the ocean. The thick walls bounded the scrubby cliff face and they could see right out to where the blue ocean met the horizon. An oil tanker was away in the distance and closer to the shore two small sailboats were ballooning across the waves. The wind blew her hair across her face and he wanted to lean in and move it, maybe trace her cheek.

'I'm glad you're enjoying present company.'

She stared out over the ocean. He could feel the wall between them again. She was very good at erecting it. An absolute expert. Darn it.

She said, 'I enjoy the company of most people.'

That showed him. 'I won't get over myself, then.' He smiled down at his hands as he stroked the round concrete cap on top of the wall. She was good for his ego. He wouldn't have one at all by the time he left here.

The stone was warm from the sun, like Ellie had been warm. Sam remembered big hands cupping her firmly, stroking. Enjoying the feel of her under his fingers too.

He could feel his body stir. She had him on the ropes just by being there. He tried to distract himself with the structure of the building. 'It's been designed well.'

'What?' She looked startled for a minute and he guessed it was too much to hope that she'd been thinking the same thing he'd been thinking. She worried at her lip and he wanted to reach out and tell her not to. He felt his fingers itch to touch that soft skin of her mouth. Gentle it. But he didn't. He kept his hands where they were because of the damn wall. Not the wall under his hands. He patted that one. He guessed he had a few walls himself.

'Yes.' She turned away from him, sent him a distracted smile still without meeting his eyes. 'I've had enough. It's getting cool. Think I'll go home and catch up on my Saturday chores. Maybe even light a fire for tonight.'

Those were his marching orders. Get your milk and go. And he was learning that, when she said enough, it meant enough. He'd love to know what the guy in her past had done to her. And maybe take him out into a dark alley and make him regret it.

Sam didn't see Ellie at all on Sunday. He thought about going up and asking for his dad's surfboard as an excuse but that was lame.

Monday and Tuesday there were no inpatients in Maternity and no births, so apart from a sociable few minutes he didn't see Ellie, who was busy with antenatal women. He was called in to a birth Trina had overnight but the woman went home as soon as the four hours were up.

By Friday he was going stir crazy. Maybe it was the wind. There were storm warnings and the ocean had been too rough to swim in this morning. He thought of her up there, with the wind howling, all by herself. Tomorrow he wouldn't even have the excuse of work to see her.

At the end of Friday's work day, late that afternoon before he left as they stood outside in the warm sunshine, he searched his brain for ideas to meet up with Ellie. She had her bag and he was jingling his keys in his pocket even though he hadn't brought his car.

He needed inspiration for an invite. 'That cyclone far north is staying nearer the coast than they thought it would.'

'So it'll be a windy night up in my cottage.' She looked higher towards her house. Clouds were building. 'I love nights when the wind creaks against the windows and you can hear the ocean smashing against the rocks below.'

'It could turn nasty.'

She looked at him as if he were crazy. Maybe he should have suggested picking up the board. He tried again. Time was running out. 'This one might be more wind than you bargain for.'

She shrugged and began walking out to the road. The intersection loomed where she'd head up to her house and he'd head down to his guesthouse. It had been a forlorn hope she'd invite him up.

Obviously that wasn't on Ellie's mind. 'The warnings come all the time. Cyclones usually veer away at the last minute. Either way, I'll be fine.'

Sam wasn't sure what had gone wrong. He'd thought they were getting along well, not too many pitfalls, but it seemed there always were pitfalls with Ellie Swift. And he kept falling into them. But there was nothing he could do except wave her goodbye. There was something about the set of her chin that warned him this wasn't a good time to ask what she was doing tomorrow. He doubted he'd be lucky enough for another set of twins to call her out.

CHAPTER NINE

OVER THE NEXT few hours the wind blew more forcefully, the trees bent and swayed under it, and branches and twigs were flying down the street in front of the hospital. Sam dropped in to see if there were any medical needs but the wards remained quiet. Maternity sat empty. Empty without Ellie.

As he battled his way back to his guesthouse he glared up towards Ellie's house. Trina had gone away for the weekend and Myra had left as well. Again. Ellie was up there completely alone.

He kept telling himself to stop it. She'd managed perfectly well without him worrying about her before. Her house was built to withstand anything the cliff tops could throw at it, and most likely she'd be offended if he asked if she wanted company. He wasn't silly enough to think she'd want to move anywhere else to take refuge.

He kept checking to see when the cyclone would veer out to the ocean and take the wind with it, but it hadn't died down at all. If anything it blew even stronger.

He drove down to the boat shed to chat to his friend, the prawn-trawler captain, and the seafarer shook his head sagely and said they were in for a 'right good blow'.

On the way back to the guesthouse, the weather warning over the radio finally clinched it.

'Cyclone Athena will hit land just north of Lighthouse Bay in less than an hour.'

That did it.

He turned the car around, drove slowly up the cliff road to Ellie's house and parked outside. He sat for a minute and looked at the other two houses, dark and deserted. He stared at Ellie's. The light behind Ellie's blinds bled into the late-afternoon gloom and the little flowering shrubs outside her door were bending in the wind.

When he opened his car door it was a struggle to climb out. The wind pushed hard and he manhandled his door open and almost lost his grip when the wind slammed into him in a gust that would have broken his arm if he'd been caught between the car and the door.

Now that would be embarrassing—coming up to help and having to be saved by Ellie. The wind pushed him towards Ellie's door like a big hand in the small of his back and he realised that it really was too dangerous to be outside in this.

Ellie only heard the knock at the door because it fell just as there was a pause in the commercial break.

Funny how she knew who it was. When she opened the door, Sam would have loomed over her in his big coat if he wasn't down one decent-sized step from her. As it was their noses were level. 'Didn't you see the weather warning?'

Nice greeting. She had no idea how but she had the

feeling he'd been stewing over something. 'No. I'm watching a movie. It's very peaceful inside!'

'The cyclone is heading this way. You can't sleep up here tonight.'

Was he for real? As he finished speaking, a sudden gust buffeted the little house and the windows creaked.

Ellie glared at Sam and narrowed her eyes. Just then a squall of rain swept sideways into Sam's back and Ellie instinctively stepped aside. 'Quickly. You'll get drenched. Come in.'

Sam bent down to take off his shoes and she dragged his arm impatiently. 'Do that in here.' As soon as he was across the threshold, she closed the door on the splattering raindrops that were making their way around his large body and onto the floor.

Sam stood on one leg and pulled his loafers off. She caught the smell of damp leather, the expensive suede mottled in places, with grass stuck to the edges from where she'd furiously cut the lawn even shorter as she'd tried to exorcise her demons earlier this afternoon.

'You've probably wrecked your shoes coming up here in them.'

His face was strangely impassive. 'Normal people don't live on cliff tops.'

What was his problem? 'Normal people leave other people alone when they've been asked to.' They were both speaking in the polite tones of people with patience tried by another's stupidity.

At that moment a fist of wind slammed solidly against the glass double doors facing the sea. The panes rattled. Then the wind sucked back fiercely before it slammed into the window again.

Ellie stopped and stared. The windows creaked and Sam placed his second loafer onto the little tray of seashells Ellie used for lining up inside shoes off the floor and he wiped the water droplets from his hair with a handkerchief.

'That's strong,' she said lamely in a normal voice.

'Really?' She could hear the exasperation in his voice. 'I couldn't leave you up here by yourself.' Sam was still speaking quietly.

'I wasn't by myself.' She indicated Myra's cat. Millicent appeared absorbed in the television and the antics of a well-dressed woman feeding cat food to a white Persian feline.

'Perfect reasoning,' he said mildly. It was infuriating he had regained equilibrium faster than she had. She'd just have to try harder.

'Would you like a cup of tea?' Politeness was good. The wind slammed against the windows again. No doubt it was slamming against her solid thick walls as well but nobody could tell that. 'My croft won't blow down, you know.'

Sam looked at the walls thoughtfully. 'I can imagine that you are correct. But it has weaknesses.' His voice lowered to an almost undistinguishable mumble. 'And obviously so do I.'

She heard him sigh as he straightened. 'I just want to make sure you…' He glanced at Millicent and corrected himself. 'You're both okay.'

He pointed to the windows. 'I seem to remember

there are shutters that close from the outside—is that right?'

Ellie had forgotten the shutters. Too late. Next time. She didn't fancy the idea of going out in that maelstrom to shut them. 'Yes, but it might be too windy to shut them now.'

Sam looked at her as if she'd grown two heads. What was his problem? 'A woman's logic.'

'Excuse me?'

As if to a child, he said, 'The shutters are there to use during extreme wind.' He spoke as if she was slow to understand. She was getting sick of his 'silly little Ellie' attitude. 'So the glass doesn't blow in?'

'The glass won't blow in.' She said it confidently. At least, the words came out confidently. Ellie had a sudden vision of glass flying all over the room. Of Millicent splattered with dangerous fragments and the wind and rain belting into the little room. Her calmness wavered. Millicent had to be safe. 'You're sure it's going to be that strong?'

Just then Ellie's feline friend disappeared and the serious voice of the weather forecaster broke into the room.

'This is an SES announcement. Severe wind warning for the north coast of New South Wales has been posted. The tail of Cyclone Athena, which had previously been expected to head out to sea, has swung back into the coast with two-hundred-kilometre winds expected right along the eastern seaboard. Residents are recommended to stay in their homes and cancel all unnecessary travel on the roads until further notice.

Flash flooding and wind damage is expected. The State Emergency Service can be reached on this number...'

A six-digit number flashed onto the screen just before the power went out.

The windows rattled menacingly in the sudden silence. Ellie stared at Sam.

He said quietly, 'Now can we close the shutters?'

'Might be a good idea.' The wind slammed again.

Sam was staring at the rain spotting the windows. 'Maybe it is too late for that. I think coming down to the hospital and staying there might be a better idea.'

As if. 'I'm not dragging Millicent through this wind. We'll be fine. But you're right. You should go before the wind gets stronger and you can't make it down the hill.'

He rolled his eyes. 'I'll do the shutters.'

No way! 'I'll do the shutters, because this is my house and I know how they fasten. And you're afraid of heights.'

He sighed, this time with exasperation. 'I'm wary of heights and more afraid that you'll blow off the cliff.'

Her eyes flew to his and the certainty in his face made her stop. He really was worried about her, to the extent he was willing to do something he normally wouldn't consider. Wayne would never have done that. The little voice inside her whispered, *Sam isn't like Wayne.* From the set chin to the determined gaze, he wasn't going to be swayed.

He lowered his voice. 'You need to stay here with Millicent.' He smiled down at the black cat who had crept across and was rubbing against Ellie's leg. He spoke to the animal. 'Can you mind Aunty Ellie while I go out and close the shutters against the wind, please?'

Millicent miaowed and Sam laughed. 'The cat wins.'

Ellie looked around. It was dark without the television.

'Fine. I'll light the lamps that I keep in the cupboard for when the silly old lights and TV go off.' She added breezily, 'It happens all the time when the wind blows strongly.'

'Do you have candles?'

She thought about Sam and her in her house, cut off from the world, with candles. 'I might.'

Ellie's face heated and she hoped he couldn't see. It was pretty dim in here. She couldn't read his eyes but she suspected they'd darkened.

Instead she went to the cupboard beside the door and took out a huge pair of black gumboots and a man's raincoat. 'These came with the house. You might still be able to salvage your loafers if you leave them to dry.'

Sam stood outside the hastily closed door, the wind buffeting him. He was mad. Obviously he still needed to feel as though he was protecting Ellie. Leftover from not protecting Bree, maybe? The wind tore at the belted raincoat and the splatter of needled rain hit his nose, and he turned his face to protect his eyes. This was dumb. Maybe they should have just let the windows blow in.

A picture of Ellie in her rain-damaged room if that did happen made his feet move and he chose to start with the worst of them first—the windows that backed onto the cliff edge. Here the force of the gale was building and he moved into it out of the lee of the building, where the full force struck him and he staggered against the wall of the building on the little porch overlooking the ocean. Ellie was looking at him from the inside with absolute horror on her face. *Great. Thanks. Very reassuring.* He managed to keep his face calm.

'Continue blowing me against the house,' he muttered. 'Happy with that.' And he kept that picture of Ellie watching him through the window in his mind to keep out the one of him being sucked off the porch and over the cliff to his death.

How had he got here? Right on the edge of a cliff in a cyclone, to be exact. Risking his life for a woman who wouldn't let him close to her. Did he hope being the hero might work when everything else hadn't?

Not that she'd wanted him to be there, and it served him right, because now he was clinging for his life, shutting oil-bereft hinges on shutters that should have been closed hours ago.

When he'd said he was more worried she would do it herself, he'd been one hundred percent telling the truth. It was that thought that drove him like a machine, unclipping, manhandling and latching each shutter closed until he was back at the side door.

He couldn't quite believe he'd been all the way around the house. It had been a real struggle, and by the end, when the wind had built to almost twice the strength from when he started, he knew Ellie would not have been able to do it.

When he fell into the room and the door was shut, he

stopped. He was dripping, gasping for breath, his face stinging from the lash of the rain, back on secure footing and out of the wind into the calm of another world. Now he felt as if…he'd come home.

CHAPTER TEN

THE ROOM WAS lit rosily. The fire Ellie kept mostly for decoration was burning merrily and Millicent was lying in front of it washing her paws. The cat barely glanced at him, she was so intent on her ablutions. *It's okay. I saved you, cat.*

But Ellie stared. Her worried face was pale, deathly pale, and he remembered the time she'd fainted, but then she flew across the room and smashed into him. She was pulling at his coat, helping him get out of his boots and then hugging him. And she buried her beautiful head in his chest. Okay. This was nice.

'That was…was dangerous. Don't do that again. I had no idea it would blow up that strong. I should never have let…' She was whispering and gabbling, Sam couldn't help thinking to himself it had all been very worth it, then, and the only way to stop her seemed perfectly reasonable to him.

He kissed her.

Sam kissed her. It was a short, cold, hard kiss, then another slower one, as if he needed to do it again, in case she'd missed the first one. She hadn't missed it. Then he hugged her. 'It's okay. I'm fine.' He spoke quietly into her hair as if she needed comfort. Darn right she needed comfort.

He tasted like the storm. It was different from the kiss they'd shared at lunch that day. Ellie hugged the wet coldness of his skin close to her. He buried her face in his damp chest, inhaling the strong scent of the sea, his aftershave and the briny tang of a man who had struggled against nature and won. For her.

He could have been blown off the cliff and she wouldn't have been able to do anything to help him. She should have gone with him, watched him, held a rope or something... It hadn't sunk into her how dangerous it was until she'd seen Sam battling to stay upright through the balcony's glass doors. She'd been so frightened for him. She'd never experienced wind like that before and even now her heart thumped at the memory.

In fact, she'd never seen someone so close to death before and that it was lovely Sam, who'd only wanted to help her, seemed ironically tragic. And she was so hard on him.

When he'd safely traversed the more dangerous face of the building she'd run around lighting candles and lighting the old fuel stove that always sat with kindling waiting in the corner of the kitchen alcove in case of blackouts. She'd set the old kettle on to heat water.

He put her away from him. 'You'll get wet. Wait until I dry and then you can cuddle me.'

She half laughed, half sobbed. 'Sorry. I got a bit emotional.' She scurried away, grabbed a towel and handed it to him. 'That was terrifying, watching you out there.'

'Tell me about it,' he said and rubbed his hair. 'It was a lot worse from where I was.' He dabbed around his neck and handed back the towel. Smiled at her. 'All good. Done now.' He glanced around and she saw the approval. 'This looks nice. Can I stay till the storm blows out?'

She looked at him. Tall. Tousled. Ridiculously handsome, yet reassuring too. The full package. Obviously he cared about her, and she wasn't stupid...she knew he fancied her. Well, heck, she fancied him too, if she was honest with herself, despite all her kicking and screaming. And he was only here for another two weeks so it wouldn't be a long-term commitment.

The wind howled and continued to build outside. 'I suppose I can't throw you out now,' she agreed a little breathlessly, happy to play down the tension of the last few minutes while he'd been outside. That had been horrible.

She remembered his car. 'Though I'm not sure how happy your lovely car will be out there with all the debris flying round.'

'There are probably less branches up here than down in the town. I'm not worried. Plus, it's there if I get called out.'

Despite the fact every birth helped her numbers and the overall viability of her plans for the hospital, she actually preferred the idea that he would not be called out. *Please.*

Ellie looked across at the stove and saw the kettle

wasn't even steaming yet. 'Are you cold? I've got the kettle on. The good news is I have pasta already cooked, and can just transfer it to an earthen dish and pop it in the fuel stove to reheat.'

He frowned. 'I've landed myself on you for dinner. I should have brought something.'

'You brought lunch the other day.' *And yourself tonight.* Her turn to look around the softly lit room. At the fire crackling. The candles. She'd pretended to herself she'd only set them because Sam had suggested them. But there was no denying the soft light added to the ambience. 'Even if the power comes on, now that I'm sorted, I like the power off.'

She suddenly felt quite calm that Sam was here. Felt strangely peaceful now she'd accepted she was attracted to him, but somehow because of the wind and the fact they were battened down here like a ship at sea in a storm it was bizarrely safe to allow herself the luxury, because it was done. He was here. She even walked across and turned off the television so it didn't blare at them in a surge when they were reconnected. She remembered the light switch and did the same to that.

It was as if some other Ellie had morphed from her body and evicted the prickly one. 'The refrigerator will make a noise when the power comes back on. That's enough to wake the dead.' The other Ellie sat down on the sofa and patted the seat beside her. 'Sit down. Rest after your efforts. Relax.' Then she thought of something. 'I've got a question.' It was a silly question but it had been bugging her.

He sat down next to her, right next to her, his hip

touching hers, and the sofa creaked with his weight. He was warm, so the coat must have worked well or he had a really good reheating system. Her mind took a little wander and she imagined what it would feel like to have a lot more of Sam's skin against hers. She wondered how much heat they could generate together. How his skin would feel? She knew from the solid impact they'd just shared, when she'd thrown herself at him like a maniac when he'd come in, that his body would be rock-solid under her hands. Her face heated and she hurriedly diverted her mad mind. The question. Yes.

After a sideways glance, Ellie decided he looked a little wary and, considering some of the questions she'd asked him, she wasn't surprised.

'I just wanted to know who taught you to make a bed with hospital corners.'

He laughed. His look said, *Is that all?* 'My mother. She was a matron, like you,' he teased. 'Met and married my dad late in life and brought us up to be "useful", as well as doctors. My sister and I were the only ones at med school who made their beds with hospital corners. We had a great childhood.'

Ellie knew his dad was a widower. 'Where is your sister now?'

His answer was easy and affectionate. 'In Italy. Doing a term of obstetrics in Rome.' Ellie could see they were still close. 'She's a workaholic.'

'Imagine. Another person striving for further knowledge.' She thought of his father. 'And your dad doesn't think of retirement? Don't you people have holidays?'

He shrugged. 'Every year when we were kids. My

parents always loved the sea, so we spent summer holidays there. Christmas at whatever beach house they'd rented for the New Year. But we always had to make our own beds.' He smiled at the memories. 'Mum and Dad adored each other until she passed away ten years ago.'

The sadness was tinged with wonderful memories. Ellie wished she had more memories of her mother. 'I'm sorry for your loss. I knew your dad was a widower.'

He smiled gently at her. 'Dad's been surfing ever since. Says it's when he feels happiest.'

Sam's smile wasn't melancholy, so she shouldn't be. 'That makes sense. He always had a smile on his face when he came in after being in the ocean.'

'So, that's my story.' He turned fully to face her. 'You owe me a little about your life, don't you think?'

'Mine's boringly tragic. As you know from my nightmares, Mum died when I was six. My dad brought me up. He never married again, though I had a nice auntie.'

She smiled at him. 'A real auntie—Dad's sister. I'd go for holidays with my Aunty Dell. She was an Outback nurse and I visited her in whatever little hospital she was working at. That was when I was happiest. I admired her so much that nursing and midwifery were the natural way for me to go. We've done a few emergency births together. She can do everything.'

He was watching her and she suddenly felt a little shy at being under such scrutiny. Wayne had asked questions about her early in their relationship, but once he'd established nobody was going to rescue her he'd stopped hearing her answers. It was something she'd missed early on and should have realised it was a danger sign.

Sam's voice brought her back and she wanted to shake off the sudden darkness that had come with thoughts of Wayne. Sam wasn't pretending interest. He *was* interested. 'So, no brothers or sisters?'

She shook her head. 'Nope.'

'And where's Aunty Dell now?'

Aunty Dell. For her, Ellie could smile. 'Kununurra. She's slowly moving around the top of Western Australia in her mobile home.'

His voice had softened. 'So no rowdy family Christmases for you?' Wayne had played on her need for 'jolly family time', and she knew it with a bitterness that stung.

Sam's face was sympathetic but she couldn't help her reaction. It erupted like a little volcano of hurt. 'Don't pity me. I've had lots of lovely Christmases at work. Making it special for people who find themselves away from home.'

Sam's expression didn't change and she took a quick breath to calm herself—remind herself this was Sam, not Wayne—and felt a little ashamed of her outburst.

He said, 'That was empathy, not pity. I can see you have a thing about pity. There's a difference. What I'd really like to know about is the relationship that's made you so bitter and prickly. It obviously didn't work out.'

Wayne hadn't been a relationship. He'd been a debilitating illness that had almost become terminal. The kettle began to sing and she heard it with relief. 'No. My relationship didn't work out.' The old Ellie was back and she stood up. 'I'll make a hot drink. Would you like tea, coffee or hot chocolate?'

He put his hand on her arm. 'Do you know what I'd really like? More than a hot drink?'

The kettle sang louder. 'What?'

Sam seemed oblivious to the noise. 'To hear about that time in your life that still affects you so much now.'

She looked down at him. Nope. She couldn't do that. She knew what would happen. Talking about Wayne and the loss of her innocence, the tearing down of her dreams, the descent into abuse she'd suffered, would spoil what she had here with Sam. Tonight couldn't be the start of a long-term thing but it was special. She wouldn't infect this moment with the past.

This thing with Sam, this fledgling, careful awareness that she was only just allowing into her world along with Sam, was too precious. Too easily damaged. 'How about you talk about your marriage first?'

'Touché.' He grimaced. She read it in his face. He knew analysing his past would harm what they had as well. 'Let's have hot chocolate instead.'

Sam sipped his hot chocolate. The fire flickered, the woman who had attracted him crazily for the first time in years sat beside him, while a big black cat purred against his side. A hell of a lot different from work, work, work. It was probably the most peaceful evening he'd spent since well before Bree's death, which was crazy, considering the tempest outside. But since he'd closed the shutters they were locked in an impervious cave, immune to the elements. There was just the rattle of rain on the roof and the background thrum of the ocean crashing on the cliffs below joining with it to make a symphony rather than a discordant refrain.

The candles flickered and as far as he was concerned Ellie looked like an angel, her cheeks slightly pink as she laughed about the time when Jeff, the lifesaver and prawn-trawler captain, the meanest, toughest guy in town, had fainted at his wife giving birth.

She turned to look at him. 'You must have had funny things happen in your work?'

'Not often.' Or maybe he'd lost his sense of humour so long ago that he'd missed the occasions. He hadn't smiled as much as he had since he'd arrived here. He wondered if it was the place or the woman beside him. He suspected it was the latter and marvelled that one person could turn his thoughts around so swiftly.

It was almost as if, the first time he'd seen her, she'd magically switched on his party lights.

She nudged him with her shoulder. 'Come on. Something funny must have happened at your work!'

He pretended to sigh. 'Very recently I was called into a birth centre and the husband was stark, staring naked in the shower with his wife and two sons while she pushed the baby out. They were from a nudist colony.'

He could tell she was trying not to laugh but he suspected it was more at his horror than the picture he painted.

She pursed her lips in mock shock. 'What about the midwife?'

He looked sternly at her. 'She was dressed. Thank goodness.'

She let go and laughed. 'You're a prude. I'm guessing

if they'd had a home birth the midwife from their colony would have been naked. Birth is such an important event that, if your belief system celebrates the naked body, I can see why they would want to be naked for it.'

He'd started the story to make her smile but she made him think more about the people, not the events. It was something he'd had trouble doing at the time and now he felt slightly ashamed. 'I'm not really complaining. The mother had had a previous caesarean, which ruled out a home birth, and they were "reclaiming her birthing ability".'

She tilted her head and looked at him. 'It's pretty cool you get that.'

He grimaced. 'I didn't get it.' He shook his head. He couldn't take credit when it wasn't due. 'I'm repeating what the midwife told me when she saw my face.'

Her gaze softened. 'But you get it now. I can see that.'

More than that had shifted since he'd come here. 'I think so.'

He tried to explain. 'I've been living a very narrow existence since Bree died. Concentrating on the end goal, which is my research on extreme premature labour. And, although it's too late to save Bree or our babies, maybe I could save other babies and somehow she'd know I was still trying.' He shook his head. 'I don't know. I've been avoiding where possible the more emotive and connecting aspects of my work. My father saw how distanced from people I was becoming so it's not surprising he saw this place as a change of scene for me.' He glanced at her ruefully. 'A chance to try to jolt me out of it.'

'And have we jolted you out of it?'

You have, he thought, but he didn't say it. He let his gaze drift around the candlelit room. Somehow it was easier to talk about it here, now, in the quiet, with just the two of them. 'I feel different. Even that first fast birth in the first half-hour here, with Josie and John. I felt connected. Involved. Not a separate watcher who only stepped in as needed.' He grimaced. 'I even recall their names.' To his shame he hadn't been able to do that for far too long.

He could see she remembered the moment. He wasn't surprised she smiled at the memory. 'You were needed.'

He shook his head. 'Not really. You had it under control. And you loved it all so much. Lived it. It slapped me in the face that I'd lost that in my work.'

She winced at his choice of words. 'Slapped? I'm definitely not a violent person.'

He smiled. 'It was a gentle, metaphorical slap. But I can change that to "nudged me into realising", if you prefer.'

He bumped her shoulder gently with his own. 'Like you nudged me to remember something funny a minute ago.'

'I'm glad you've seen the light.' She said it simply.

'And since then it's been a roller coaster. Lighthouse Bay doesn't win the birth number-count but every patient has had a story, an emotional tag I'm seeing now. That's a good thing. I think.'

She touched his arm. 'It's definitely a good thing.'

That wasn't all he was seeing. He was seeing a beautiful woman, just out of reach. He really wanted to reach. He just hoped she was also feeling the magic that had snared him.

'Come here.' He lifted his arm and to his immense relief she snuggled in under the weight of it. Then it was easy to tilt her chin with his other hand and brush her lips with his. He could feel the tingle of connection all the way down to his toes. He sighed and suddenly felt ten years younger. Now he was alive.

Ellie had known they were going to kiss. Eventually. And surprisingly she was quite calm about it. It wasn't as if they hadn't before and he was very good at it. That other Ellie was stretching inside her and saying, *Yes, please*, as Sam pulled her close. *Hurry up and kiss me some more*, that other Ellie was saying. She was such a hussy.

His mouth touched hers. Mmm… Kissing Sam tasted crazy good. Strangely their bodies were communing like two old lovers—not new ones—and inexplicably she once again found herself in his lap. She kept her eyes closed dreamily as she slid her arms around his strong neck and savoured the virile hardness and warmth of him. The slowness and languorous progression of his mouth from gentle to intense, hard to soft, and back again. It felt so powerful with him holding her face, her cheeks, cradled between his palms as if he held delicate china in his hands. Tasting her and letting her taste him. As though she was precious and special. Breathing in each other's breath as they shared the most intimate connection with their mouths.

Distantly she heard the rain beat on the roof and the

spiral of delight just went on, deeper and more poignantly, until she wanted to cry with the beauty of his mouth against hers, his tongue curled around hers, until her whole body seemed to glow from the inside out. Kissing and more kissing. She hadn't realised she could love kissing this much. That kissing was actually the be all and end all. That it could be a whole play and not just an act of the play. She'd never been kissed like this—as if he couldn't get enough of her mouth. His hands roamed, as if gathering her even closer, but always they came back to her face, gently holding her mouth to his as if he couldn't get enough. Yes. She couldn't get enough, either.

Sam was staying the night. Tomorrow was Saturday. They had all night—or even all weekend, if they wanted.

He stayed all weekend. Sunday morning, she woke to the warmth of Sam's big naked body snug up against her and her cheek on Sam's skin. The blond hairs on his body tickled her nose and her hand closed over the wedge-shaped muscle of his chest as her face grew steadily pinker. Oh, my. What they had done since Friday night?

As if he'd heard her thoughts, his voice announced he was awake too. 'I'm wondering if perhaps we could do some of that again…'

Sam's voice was a seductive rumble and she could feel the smile curve across her face. No doubt she looked like Millicent after scoring a treat. She knew now what Trina was missing and why the young widow had chosen to work most nights. Waking to someone warm and loving beside her. A man spoiling her until she begged him to stop. Being held until she fell asleep.

Cheeks still red, she tried to not jump on him. 'Aren't you hungry?'

'Oh, yeah, I'm starving.' He pulled her on top of him and kissed her thoroughly.

An hour later Ellie watched the steam follow Sam out of the bathroom and ran her hands slowly over her tingling body. She'd had no idea such a sensuous world existed, though how on earth she was going to face Sam at work and not think lurid thoughts defied her imagination. Sam had told her to stay and enjoy the shower while he made breakfast but what she really wanted to do was drag the gorgeous person back to bed. She'd had no idea she was a nymphomaniac. Must be. Surely other people didn't do it so much as they had in the last thirty-six hours?

She didn't know how it could work between them. If it even could work. He was based in Brisbane. She was here. But they were fabulous together so surely that meant something? Maybe she could learn to trust a relationship with a man. A long-distance relationship. If that man was Sam. No. She wasn't in love with him. Was she? She wasn't going there, but she sure as heck was in lust with him.

And if it didn't work long-distance, that was okay, because he would only be here for another two weeks and she deserved great sex at least once in her life. More than once. She grimaced over the word. They hadn't had sex—Sam had made love to her. Gloriously tender love that healed and nurtured and told her he thought she was the sexiest woman in the world. Who would have known? Her cheeks glowed again.

CHAPTER ELEVEN

MONDAY MORNING DAWNED, blustery, and Ellie tweaked her collar tighter to her throat as she closed her front door. She'd slept deeply after Sam had left on Sunday evening. They'd walked for hours hand in hand along Nine Mile Beach, splashing through the waves, coming back after lunch ravenous again. Ellie was convinced that the sun, the exercise and—she grinned to herself—the loving meant she'd slept the best she'd slept for years.

This morning the air felt damp and exhilarating as she trod lightly down the road to work just before seven a.m. She'd skipped her beach walk this morning—strangely, her hips were tender. Must be all the exercise. She blushed sheepishly.

The sea remained wild, white caps out to the horizon, booming swells smashing against the cliff below, and Ellie breathed in the fresh salt with a sigh of pleasure. She loved the coast. Loved the isolation of her croft, though isolation wasn't something she'd savoured over the weekend. She saw Myra's car was back and smiled to herself. She didn't know. *Tee-hee.*

She laughed out loud and conversely had a sudden desire to share the amusing thought with Sam. There was a little wonky logic in that thought and it was not very loyal to her friend.

On her arrival she saw that Trina had had a slow night. The ward remained empty. Her friend had been bored, hence she had reorganised the whole sterile stockroom—a job Ellie had been putting off until a quiet day—and there was a small pile of out-of-date stock that she needed to reorder from the base hospital. At least she had a chore to start her day with.

Later, if no birthing women came in or needed transfer, Ellie would do the same for the medication cupboard. Spring cleaning suited the feeling of determined efficiency she'd decided she needed to ground herself in. Get her head out of the clouds that her thoughts kept drifting up towards.

The expected arrival of Dr Southwell would not faze her, though seriously she wouldn't be able to look at him without blushing, and she wasn't sure how she was going to manage it.

Maybe, as they had no patients, he could go straight through to the clinic in the main hospital to give her a chance to think of what to say.

Except it wasn't Sam who arrived.

Wayne Donnelly was an undeniable presence. Like everyone's favourite young uncle. You could just imagine him dangling babies on his knees, which was what Ellie had thought when he'd begun to pursue her. Whenever Ellie was around he'd made such a fuss of any child and everyone had smiled at him. He'd made her think of families. Dream families. Christmases, Easter egg hunts. All the things Ellie had ever wanted, and she'd fallen headlong in love with the fantasy.

In truth, he hated kids, and was a narcissist and a sociopath. He had no guilt, no shame, no feeling for other people, and could only see the world through eyes that saw himself first.

But he was like a seasoned politician versed in the art of crowd pleasing. Crinkled laughter lines jumped up at the edges of blue eyes framed by thick, black lashes and high cheekbones. Nothing in his looks gave him away. Except maybe the confident, beaming, too-white smile. He had a small cleft in his strong chin and women instinctively gave him another look.

Later she'd found out there was a pattern. He serenaded his victims, pretended to marry them, created joint bank accounts and then sauntered off after skilfully denigrating the woman so she felt it was all her fault everything had failed. A master of psychological abuse.

When Ellie saw him her stomach lurched with bile. Out of the corner of her eye she saw Trina, about to head home to bed, instinctively pat her hair. Yep. He'd already sucked in Trina.

'What are you doing here?' Ellie watched his smile broaden, the fake smile he used like oil to smooth his way in so he could use someone. She'd been incredibly blind. She wasn't any more.

'Too early in the morning for manners, El? Introduce me to your beautiful friend before we find ourselves bickering.'

'No.' Ellie turned from him to Trina. 'He's a cad and a slime, Trina. I'd leave if I was you.'

Wayne laughed. Trina looked at Ellie and shut her gaping mouth with a click. She blinked a few times as her tired brain tried to work it out. Then she stepped closer to Ellie. 'If you say so, I believe you.'

Ironic choice of words from her friend. One of the people in the room was a huge liar.

Trina frowned. 'But…' She wrinkled her brow. 'If he's a cad shouldn't I stay?'

Ellie shook her head. 'I'd prefer you didn't. He won't be here long. You could ring the security man, though. Ask him to come over and sit at my desk. That would be good in case he won't leave.'

Trina didn't look again at Ellie's acquaintance, just crossed to the desk and picked up the phone. She spoke quietly into it and then picked up her bag. 'If you're sure.'

Ellie nodded again. 'Please. And thanks.'

Trina nodded. 'See you tomorrow morning.'

'Sure.' Ellie Looked back at Wayne. Raised her brows. 'Yes?'

'I need money.'

'Really.' He had taken a great deal of that from her already. Along with her naivety. She looked at the impeccable clothes. 'I've seen people far worse off than you.'

'Thank you.' As if she'd given him a wonderful compliment. 'Nice little caravan park you have here. Think I might stay around for a while. Reacquaint myself with my kin.'

'You have no kin. But I can't stop you. Luckily, it's high season and will cost you an arm and a leg. So you will have to move on eventually.' She wasn't moving on. Not this time.

He spread his hands. 'Gambling debts.'

Nothing new. 'Gamblers tend to get those.'

'This time they threatened to harm my family.'

He'd had three 'wives' that she knew of. 'Which family?'

'All of them. You included. I thought I'd better warn you.'

He didn't give a damn. 'You don't care about anyone but yourself. You'd do better going to the police.'

'I don't think that the police station is a safe place for me to go. Would you look forward to identifying my body?'

'Go away, Wayne. Your disasters have nothing to do with me.' And she could feel the shakes coming on. He'd tried to rape her once. After she'd said she was leaving him. And he'd denied it. Said she'd been playing hard to get.

She'd escaped that night and had begun to plan carefully to get away, because he'd taken all her resources. Her wallet, her licence, her bank accounts... Everything had been unavailable when she'd needed it. She'd stumbled into Myra's coffee shop, distraught, and made a friend for life. Myra had helped her create the wall of protection she needed to be free.

'You've turned all bitter and twisted. Not the sweet Ellie I used to know.'

That wasn't even worth answering. Ellie heard the

door from the main hospital open and was glad the security guard was here. She needed to end this. She pretended she didn't know help had arrived. She couldn't keep running.

'Leave the ward, please, Mr Donnelly.'

'You didn't call me "Mr Donnelly" when we were married.'

'We were never married.' Ellie turned away from him to the security guard and her stomach dropped. It wasn't security, it was Sam. No. No. *No.* Her face flushed and she felt dreadfully, horribly sick. She didn't want Sam to know about this. But then maybe it was best. Then he could see she could never truly give a man power over her ever again.

'Good morning, matron,' Sam said.

Ellie saw him glance at Wayne and give him an inscrutable nod. 'We need to discuss the patients.' Sam's voice was surprisingly crisp. Authoritative. No hint of friendliness.

Ellie raised her brows. He knew there were no patients. 'Certainly, Dr Southwell.'

'Fine. When you're ready, please.'

'She's busy. Talking to me.' Wayne squared his shoulders but he was at a disadvantage in both height and muscle. They all knew it. An adolescent part of Ellie secretly revelled in it.

Still politely, Sam said, 'You're a doctor?'

'No. I'm her...'

Before Wayne could complete his sentence, Sam spoke coldly right over the top of him. There was no doubting his authority. 'This is a hospital. If you are not a medical practitioner, matron's attention is mine. There is a waiting room, though, in the main hospital where you can sit, but this could take some time.'

Ellie added helpfully, 'He's leaving.'

'Excellent. Come with me, matron.' Sam indicated with his hand that he expected Ellie to head down the corridor to the empty rooms in front of him.

She looked at Wayne and made the decision to enforce her freedom from dreaded drop-in visits like this. She didn't know why she hadn't done it before but knew it was a fault she needed to remedy immediately. 'If you don't leave town, I'll lodge a restraining order with the police this afternoon. I've kept evidence of our fake marriage certificate. This won't happen again.'

Then she turned to Sam. 'This way, doctor.'

Sam ignored Wayne and followed Ellie. She could feel his large body blocking Wayne's view of her as they turned into an empty room and stood silently in the centre of it out of sight. Ellie clasped her hands together to stop them shaking, unable to look at Sam. They both heard footsteps retreating, and the automatic doors open and close, and Ellie sagged against a wall. Sam watched her but he didn't come any closer, as if he knew she needed space at this moment.

'Your ex-husband, I assume?'

'He was a bigamist. Or trigamist, if there is such a word. So never legally my husband.'

Sam whistled. 'Ouch.'

She said very quietly, 'There were worse things about him than that.'

Sam studied her. 'Would you like me to follow and punch him out?'

He was deadly serious. She could see that.

She could almost smile at that except her heart was broken. Yes, she was beginning to love Sam. That was so dangerous to her peace of mind. It frightened the stuffing out of her. And she loved him even more for the offer, but Wayne had made her see how impossible it all was. She couldn't do this—start again with Sam. She didn't have the trust in her to build a strong relationship and Sam needed a woman to love him wholeheartedly.

Not one who'd locked him out like Bree had. Bree, who had almost destroyed him while she'd destroyed herself. He deserved that trust. She could give him love. She was more than halfway to falling in love with him already. But she couldn't give him trust. She'd thought she could but she couldn't. Trust had died in her for ever. Killed by the man who had just left.

'Thank you for the thought but I wouldn't like to ask you to sink to his level.' She straightened off the wall.

'Now you can see, Sam, why I'm so wary of men. Why I know I'll never let myself get that close to someone again. I'm sorry if I gave you the wrong idea this weekend. It was lovely, what we shared, but it's finished. You'll leave soon and that's good.' She took a step towards the door and it was the hardest step she'd ever taken. 'Let's go back to the desk.'

His fingers lifted to touch her arm, then dropped. 'Ellie.'

'Yes?' She looked at his caring eyes. His beautiful

mouth. The kindness that shone on his face. It broke her heart.

'I'm sorry you've been wounded by a pathetic man. We're not all like that.'

She heard him. Saw that he meant it. But that didn't help. She wished she could believe it as deeply as she needed to be fair to Sam. 'I know. I really don't think you are that sort of man, but I don't have the capacity in me to risk a relationship again. A relationship needs to be good for both of us and I wouldn't be good for you.'

'But—'

She cut him off. 'Thank you. I don't want to talk about it any more.'

Sam sighed impatiently. 'I can understand that here. But later, I think we should.'

'No, Sam. We won't.' Then she turned and walked away.

Sam left Ellie soon after. He went out the front door to make sure her ex-bigamist had departed but there was no sign of him. He actually would have liked to slam the sleazy little mongrel up against a wall and warn him never to approach Ellie again, but he might find a place in himself that would do more than that, and he'd taken an oath to not harm.

His fingers clenched by his sides. No wonder she had trust issues and didn't want to ask any man for help. Even himself. He wasn't a violent man but after what they'd shared the last two days the idea of someone abusing Ellie's trust to that extent devastated him. And made him furious. But in the end it wasn't any of his business unless he was looking for something long-term—which wasn't his intention. Or was it? Hell, he didn't know. Did he even have a choice?

Ellie spent the next five days rearranging antenatal schedules and managed to book a different pregnant woman for antenatal appointments for every morning during the time Sam would be around.

They had two normal births, one on Faith's shift and one on Trina's, so Ellie was spared having to call Sam in. She could only be glad the babies were being kind to her. But every afternoon when she went home the house was empty, where before it had been welcoming.

Sam came on Wednesday afternoon for his father's surfboard and she gave it to him, refused to talk and didn't invite him in.

On Thursday Myra cornered her and told her Sam had asked her to see if Ellie would change her mind. Spend some time with him. They had their first ever disagreement when both women were so determined to change the other's mind about what was right.

By Friday Ellie knew she needed to get away or she would make herself sick, so as soon as she finished work she took herself off availability for call-backs and loaded her car.

Ellie felt the need to abandon her cottage and head to a different world. It had everything to do with avoiding a certain visitor who just might drop in again.

She didn't know where to go, so she drove north to the Gold Coast, where she could find a cheap hotel and just hibernate for two nights in a place that no-body knew her.

She stayed in her room all day Saturday and drove back Sunday via the base hospital where two of her patients were still inpatients.

She did her own visiting, with a quiet chat in the big antenatal ward with Marni, who was going home to-morrow. Bob arrived not long after she did, and she was pleased to hear that the young mum's contractions had settled down, and Bob had painted inside their house while Marni was in hospital so she didn't have to be exposed to the smell of new paint.

She showed Ellie the quilt she was making the baby, and there was something about Marni's determined optimism that made her feel ashamed. Marni had explained that when she was bored she sewed another little animal onto the patchwork cot-blanket, pouring love and calmness into it, determined to do everything asked of her to keep her pregnancy on track.

After Marni, Ellie visited the postnatal ward area, where Annette sat happily with her twins, who were being star patients and were almost ready to go home.

'Still perfect?' Ellie grinned at the two sleeping bundles and the relaxed mum sitting with a magazine in her lap.

'They have their moments. Rosebud is the impatient one, so has to be fed first, while Thorn needs a bit of encouragement to keep at it.'

'So they are still how they started out, then.'

'Exactly.' Both women laughed.

'How is that gorgeous Dr Sam?'

'Fine.' Ellie felt her face freeze, as if all the muscles had suddenly stopped working. 'He's here for another week and then he's gone.' Her voice was bright. 'Then I guess we'll have another new locum. Did you know his father was here first? He was a surfer, though I'm not sure how good his surfing will be for a while, because he broke his arm. That's why his son came.'

'So Dr Sam's not coming back?'

'No.' It would be better if Sam never came back. She suspected every time he came it would hurt more to keep saying goodbye to him. 'He has a high-flying job in Brisbane. He was only doing everyone a favour.' Including her.

On the drive home she thought about her dilemma. She'd had sex with a man she'd known for only two weeks by that point, and who was just passing through. Maybe she even understood her friend Faith, who had never said she regretted the man who'd come, disappeared and left her with a baby. She'd never been close to understanding before.

Sex. She grimaced and reminded herself that that was all it was. Then her sensible voice returned. That was okay. She was a grown-up. Afterwards she could go back to how it had been before and concentrate on work.

On Monday morning when Sam walked in to the maternity ward the Ellie he found was the woman from three weeks ago. White shirt buttoned to the neck, grey eyes serene and cool, her manner very businesslike.

'Good morning, doctor.'

His temper was less than sunny after being frustrated all weekend. He'd thought if he just waited until Saturday morning they could sort it all out. He'd taken croissants and blueberry yoghurt, as she'd liked that last time, and then had stood there like an idiot until he'd realised she'd left. He'd rung Myra each morning and afternoon all weekend to check in case she'd returned.

Now he stared with narrowed eyes as she stood officiously in front of him. 'Good morning, Ellie.' He stressed her first name, disappointed but not surprised this ice maiden didn't resemble the woman he had held in his arms all weekend just over a week ago. He was back to square one, and despite his best efforts there was no breaking through her barriers. Maybe he should just give up.

They had five days to go. Then he'd be gone. He could lose himself in his work again. Treat it as an interlude that had shown him he could finally care for another woman. But he wasn't so sure he could care for one as much as he'd grown to care for Ellie.

On Friday morning, Sam's last day there, Ellie went back to the beach. She'd been avoiding it all week in case Sam was there in the mornings surfing but she missed the peace she gained from her daily walk. Peace was at a premium at the moment and she needed it before facing today.

It had rained last night, and the ocean was too rough for surfers out there. As she trod down the path even the frogs weren't penetrating the gloom she was wrapped in. At least she had Sam to thank for losing the majority of her phobia. She wasn't going to touch one but the

croaking barely bothered her now—there were worse
things that could happen than frogs. Such as Sam going
and never seeing him again.

She reached the sand, slipped off her footwear and
stood for a moment. Gazing out. A new weather pattern
was coming in. More high winds and rough seas. She
breathed in deeply and let the crash of the waves on the
cliffs across the bay penetrate, feeling the cool white
sand between her toes, the turbulent, curving waves
tumbling onto themselves and running up the sand to
kiss her better. The biggest waves made a cracking noise
as they slid all the way up to her to foam around her
toes then crackle into the sand as it drank in the water
and the cries of the gulls overhead. This was why she
lived here. Because it made her strong.

Yes, it was sad that Sam was going, more than sad,
but it was good as well. It would never have worked
and what he'd given her in the two days they'd been
together was something she could hold to her heart in
the years to come. She wished him happiness with a
woman who deserved him. She just wished she could
have been that woman.

Ellie lifted her head and breathed in another gulp of
sea air past the stinging in her throat and then she set
off along the beach. She would get through today, kiss
Sam's cheek and say goodbye.

Sam knew she was going to kiss his cheek. He didn't
want her platonic guilt. If she wasn't going to kiss him
properly then he didn't want her to kiss him at all. He

stepped back as she moved forward to say goodbye and saw her blink in confusion as he avoided her.

That's right, Ellie. Feels bad, doesn't it, to be knocked back? He didn't say it but he knew it was there in his eyes. He was still pretty darn angry with her for not fighting for what they might have had.

'Goodbye, Ellie Swift. I wish you a great life with your midwifery centre.' He turned away quickly because if he didn't he'd grab her and kiss her until she begged him to stay. But that wouldn't happen.

He'd driven an hour towards Brisbane when the radio alert of another storm warning jerked him back to sense. Ellie was on the seaboard. Right on the edge of a cliff, to be exact. Her little house would bear the brunt of the storm and he wouldn't be there to make sure she was all right.

Not that she'd want him to be there, but suddenly he asked himself why would he drive away from a woman who'd finally made him want to look at the future again? One he wanted to wake up next to for the rest of his life? He loved Ellie. How many times did real love actually come to a man?

After he'd stepped back from her he'd seen the look of hurt on her face and it came back to haunt him now. What if she was feeling the same pain he was? Wasn't he as bad as she was for not fighting for what they could have?

He'd loved Bree, and it had destroyed him when she'd died. But Ellie was right. It hadn't been his fault. He didn't know she'd been so unstable that she would take her own life. And he'd lost himself in work.

If it wasn't for Lighthouse Bay and Ellie he might be still lost. He could have woken up in thirty years and realised he'd been a shell for decades. He didn't want to be a shell. He wanted to be the man who held Ellie every night. The man who held the babies she was destined to have with him, and might never have if he kept driving away. He loved her. He wanted her. And he would fight for her.

He pulled over and turned around. The storm up ahead was flashing lightning across the hills. Great sheets of white light. Ellie was over there somewhere. Alone.

The thunder crashed outside. The scent of ozone filled the air, lighting up the sky all the way out to sea. This storm was more electrical than the other one. She shied away from those memories of the night Sam came, like Millicent had skidded away from the window.

Myra was gone again and Ellie suspected she had a male friend she was visiting. She even suspected it might be the 'elder' Dr Southwell. Good for her.

But Ellie knew the man she should have fought for was gone. Sam was gone. In her head he was gone. In her heart he was buried under protection so thick she felt like she was walking around inside a big, white cotton-wool ball, adding more layers all week, so that by the time Sam had left this afternoon she could barely hear, she was so distanced from everyone. He'd turned away from her coldly in the end and she deserved that. She'd been a coward and deserved his scorn.

She wished she'd never ever started this painful process of letting someone else in. Because for the first time in a long time she wondered if, if she'd tried a little bit harder to let go of the past, she just might have had a future. With Sam. Was it too late? Could she contact him through his father? Myra would be all over her like a rash if she asked for Sam's phone number. Or his flat address. Maybe she could turn up at his flat. Her heart began to pound and she looked down at Millicent. 'Am I mad to think of it or mad not to do it, cat?'

She had a sudden memory of Marni, determined to fight for her baby. Shoring herself up with positive actions. Stitching her quilt of love so that she would be ready when the good things happened. Ellie had done the opposite, undermined her own confidence with the past every time Sam broke through her barriers.

Stop it. Too late, it's over. She stroked the soft fur between Millicent's pointy ears.

She sat up straight. 'You know what, Milly? It's not over till the fat lady sings. I'll find him tomorrow and see if we can at least spend some time together.' She would try and, if it didn't work out, then she might just have to get a cat of her own. Maybe a kitten so she could have the full experience of being a mother. Yeah, right. Full experience.

The knock came in between two claps of thunder and she frowned at the improbability of visitors.

Then, there was Sam. Standing on the bottom step, his nose level with hers, his dark eyes staring into hers.

'Can I come in?' A flash of lighting illuminated them both and a nearby tree exploded into sparks. The explosion made her ears ring and she put out her hand to drag him in.

'Damn it, Sam. You could get killed standing out in that. You're mad.' Her heart was thumping at the closeness of the strike and the concept that again she could have got Sam killed by keeping him outside her house.

Then he was inside, the door was shut and they both stood there, panting, a few inches of air and a huge chasm between them.

He didn't seem perturbed about what had almost happened. He just said softly, 'You haven't closed the shutters again.'

She couldn't believe he was here. As if she'd conjured him. 'I know. It's not that windy. And you can't do it because it's too dangerous to go out in case the lightning gets you.' She licked her dry lips. 'Why are you here, Sam?'

He was staring down at her. She couldn't read the expression in his eyes but it was nothing like the one he'd left with today. It was warm, gentle and determined. 'Can I share the storm with you?'

Her cheeks were heating. He looked so good. Smelt so good. She knew he would feel so good. 'That would be nice,' she said carefully.

His brows rode up. 'Nice?' He put down his coat. 'It could be more than nice. Because I've decided to fight for you.'

This was all happening way too fast for her to erect the barriers she needed. Hang on—she didn't need barriers. Her brain was fogging. Softening. Revelling in the fact that Sam was here.

Sam said, 'I'm going to wear you down until you say yes.'

He wasn't gone. She hadn't ruined everything. Yet! Then his words sank in. 'Yes to what?'

'Will you marry me, Ellie? Be my wife. We'll work out the logistics—our work, your fears, my baggage. But driving away from you today and knowing I wasn't coming back was the loneliest thing I've ever done in my life, and I don't want to do it again. I love you.'

He loved her. 'Oh, Sam.' She loved him. Lord, she loved him so much. She lifted her head. She loved him too much to push him away for a second time. She would just have to break free from the past and be everything Sam needed. For the sake of both their futures. 'I love you too.'

He closed his eyes. 'It was too close, Ellie. We were too close to losing this.' Then he stepped in and picked her up. Hugged her to him and swung her around. And she laughed out loud. Sam's arms had her. They both were laughing and then he kissed her, and Ellie knew, at last, that she had found her 'for ever' family.

CHAPTER TWELVE

SAM STOOD WAITING, his heart pounding as he watched for the first signs of the bridal car to descend the gravel road to the beach, and he appreciated the grounding effect of the cool sand under his bare feet as he waited for the warmth of the sun. But, more impatiently, he waited for the glowing warmth of the woman he would spend the rest of his life with. Where was Ellie?

The light touch of a hand on his arm broke into his thoughts and he turned with a smile to his father. He saw the old man's eyes were damp and shadowed with that memory of past sadness, yet glowing with pride too. Happy and sad at the same moment. Sam knew all about that. They both glanced at Sam's sister as she stood with her Italian friends, back on sabbatical to her old hospital while she attended her only brother's wedding.

His dad cleared his throat and said quietly, 'Your mother would have been so proud of you, son. So happy for you.'

Sam patted his shoulder. Felt the sinewy strength under his hand and was glad his dad was healed again.

'She'd be happy for you too. We've both been blessed twice with wonderful women.'

'I can see you love your Ellie, Sam.'

Sam felt his face relax, felt his mind expand with just thinking about her. Felt the joy surge up into his chest. Such elation. 'She's turned the world on for me, Dad. Ellie, this place, the future.' He shook his head, still unable to believe his grey life had been hit by a sunburst called Ellie Swift. Soon to be Mrs Southwell. 'I just wish she'd hurry up and arrive.'

The first rays of the sunrise struck the cliff in front of them at the exact moment an old-fashioned black saloon descended the steep slope and finally drew up at the place reserved for the bride in the crowded car park.

The whole town had come out in the dark to wait for the sunrise and for Ellie. The dapper chauffer, not resembling a prawn-trawler captain at all, opened the door onto a long blue roll of carpet that reached all the way across the sand to Sam.

He helped the two golden bridesmaids in their beautiful sheath dresses, Trina and Faith, and the stately Matron of Honour in a vintage gold dress, his dad's fiancée, Myra, and then Sam heard the hushed gasp from a town full of supporters as Ellie stepped out in a vision of white with her father's hand in hers.

Ellie had been shy about a veil, a white dress, the fact that she'd thought she was a bride before and had been mistaken, but Sam had taken her in his arms and told her his dream…of Ellie on the beach dressed as a bride. Sam had spoken quietly of the pureness of their love, the freshness of their commitment and his desire for her to feel the bride of her dreams—because their life together would be that dream.

And there she was, drifting towards him, the veil dancing at the sides of her face in the morning breeze, walking a little too quickly in her bare feet as she always did, her eyes on his, her smile wide and excited as she closed the gap between them. She came first, not after the bridesmaids, almost dragging her dad, and Sam was glad, because he could watch her close the gap between them all the way, and he barely saw the three smiling women behind her. He'd told them he wasn't talking to them anyway—they'd kept his Ellie at Myra's house last night sequestered away from him. They and her Aunty Dell, back from Western Australia for her only niece's wedding.

When Ellie stopped in front of him her eyes were glowing behind the fine material of the veil and he took her hand in his and felt the tension drain from his shoulders like an eddy rushing from a freshly filled rock pool. Ellie's dad released his daughter's hand, smiled wistfully and waved them on.

The sun chose that moment to break free of the ocean and bathed the whole wedding party in golden-pink rays as they rearranged themselves in front of the minister. The crowd drew closer, the waves pounded on the rocks by the cliff, Sam's hand tightened on Ellie's and the ceremony began, accompanied by the sound of the gulls overhead.

Afterwards the wedding breakfast was set out on white-cloth-covered tables on the long veranda of the surf

club restaurant that looked out over the bay. The local
Country Women's Association ladies had whipped up a
magnificent repast and Ellie's new husband kept catching her eye with such love, such devotion and pride, she
constantly fought back happy tears which she refused
to let free. Not now. Not today. She had never thought
she could be this happy.

She touched the sleeve of his white tuxedo coat.
'Sam, let's take a minute to ourselves. Walk with me
on the beach.' She watched his face soften, saw it glow
with love and pride, and those blinking tears that had
stung her eyes threatened again. She willed them away.

So they turned down the steps of the surf club, away
from the revelries, and people parted smilingly and
nudged each other. 'Let them go. Young lovers.'

Finally it was just Ellie and Sam walking along the
beach, barefoot in the morning sunlight, Ellie's dress
hitched over her arm, toes making fresh footprints in
virgin sand, and every now and then the froth of the
chuckling waves tickled their ankles.

'I love you, Sam.'

'I love you too, my wife.'

She hugged the words to herself and used them to
make her brave. She had news and she wanted to share
it but they hadn't had a moment together alone all morning.

'This morning...' she began, and felt the nerves well.
Hoped desperately he would be glad. 'This morning,
I did a test.'

His big, dark brows, those brows she loved and traced

at night with her fingers, drew together. He didn't get it. 'And did you pass your test?'

'It was positive.'

She let the words hang suspended with the sound of the sea between them. Squeezed his hand in hers and waited. Felt his fingers still beneath hers.

'Pregnant?' His voice was almost a whisper.

Her heart squeezed and she nodded. 'Our baby. Just weeks in time, but it feels good. The feeling is right. Everything will be fine, Sam.' She stopped and turned to him, took his face in hers instead of the other way around. Felt the skin of his cheeks tense as he realised what she'd been trying to tell him 'My darling, everything will be perfect.'

His face stilled and then slowly, ever so slowly, he smiled. It rose from somewhere so deep inside him that she was blinded by the joy she had been so afraid would be missing, consumed instead by fear that what had happened to Bree would happen to her too.

He smiled, then he grinned, picked her up and swung her around as if she were a feather, and then he hugged her. Fiercely. Put her down. Glanced around and then picked her up again. Laughed out loud. Ellie was giddy with relief, giddy with swinging, giddy with Sam.

The only minor glitch would be the time she spent on maternity leave.

But Lighthouse Bay Mothers and Babies would be fine. Sam had taken the post of Director of Obstetrics at the base hospital an hour away and his father had become the permanent GP for Lighthouse Bay. Soon Ellie would have the midwifery service she dreamed of, because now she had a straight pathway of referral to a higher level of service if needed. She knew the obstetrician in charge—her new husband—very well, and he was extremely supportive. And in the wings was Trina, ready to come off night duty and take over when Ellie stepped down. And after her there was Faith, and then Roz, and other midwives waiting to be a part of the journey travelled by the midwives of Lighthouse Bay.

* * * * *

*If you enjoyed this story,
check out these other great reads
from Fiona McArthur*

*MIDWIFE'S MISTLETOE BABY
MIDWIFE'S CHRISTMAS PROPOSAL
CHRISTMAS WITH HER EX
GOLD COAST ANGELS: TWO TINY HEARTBEATS*

All available now!

MILLS & BOON®

**MEDICAL
ROMANCE**

THE ULTIMATE IN ROMANTIC MEDICAL DRAMA

A sneak peek at next month's titles...

In stores from 23rd March 2017:

- **Their One Night Baby** – Carol Marinelli *and*
  Forbidden to the Playboy Surgeon – Fiona Lowe

- **A Mother to Make a Family** – Emily Forbes *and*
  The Nurse's Baby Secret – Janice Lynn

- **The Boss Who Stole Her Heart** – Jennifer Taylor *and*
  Reunited by Their Pregnancy Surprise – Louisa Heaton

Just can't wait?
Buy our books online before they hit the shops!
www.millsandboon.co.uk

Also available as eBooks.

0317/03

MILLS & BOON®

EXCLUSIVE EXTRACT

Dr. Dominic MacBride had no intention of falling in love—yet now he's fighting for paramedic Victoria Christie...and their surprise baby!

Read on for a sneak preview of
THEIR ONE NIGHT BABY

'You got your earring back.'

'They were a gift from my father.'

'That's nice,' Dominic said.

'Not really, it was just a duty gift when I turned eighteen. Had he bothered to get to know me, then he'd have known that I don't like diamonds.'

'Why not?'

'I don't believe in fairytales and I don't believe in for ever.'

There was, to Victoria's mind, no such thing.

She held her breath as his fingers came to her cheek and lightly brushed the lobe as he examined the stone.

If it were anyone else she would have pushed his hand away.

Anyone else.

Yet she provoked.

'It was the other earring that I lost.'

And he turned her face and his hands went to the other.

This was foolish, both knew.

Neither wanted to get close to someone they had to

work alongside but the attraction between them was intense.

Both knew the reason for their rows and terse exchanges; it was physical attraction at its most raw.

'Victoria, I'm in no position to get involved with anyone.'

They were standing looking at each other and his hands were on her cheeks and his fingers were warm on her ears. There was a thrum between them and she knew he was telling her they would go nowhere.

'That's okay.'

And that *was* okay.

'If you don't like diamonds, then what do you like?' he asked. His mouth was so close to hers and though it was cold she could feel the heat in the space between them.

'This.'

Their mouths met and she felt the warm, light pressure and it felt blissful.

Don't miss
THEIR ONE NIGHT BABY
By Carol Marinelli

Available April 2017
www.millsandboon.co.uk

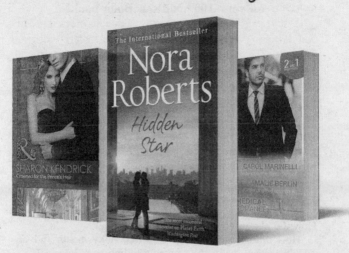

MILLS & BOON®

Congratulations
Carol Marinelli
on your 100th Mills & Boon book!

Read on for an exclusive extract

How did she walk away? Lydia wondered.

How did she go over and kiss that sulky mouth and say goodbye when really she wanted to climb back into bed?

But rather than reveal her thoughts she flicked that internal default switch which had been permanently set to 'polite'.

'Thank you so much for last night.'

'I haven't finished being your tour guide yet.'

He stretched out his arm and held out his hand but Lydia didn't go over. She did not want to let in hope, so she just stood there as Raul spoke.

'It would be remiss of me to let you go home without seeing Venice as it should be seen.'

'Venice?'

'I'm heading there today. Why don't you come with me? Fly home tomorrow instead.'

There was another night between now and then, and Lydia knew that even while he offered her an extension he made it clear there was a cut-off.

Time added on for good behaviour.

And Raul's version of 'good behaviour' was that there would

be no tears or drama as she walked away. Lydia knew that. If she were to accept his offer then she had to remember that.

'I'd like that.' The calm of her voice belied the trembling she felt inside. 'It sounds wonderful.'

'Only if you're sure?' Raul added.

'Of course.'

But how could she be sure of anything now she had set foot in Raul's world?

He made her dizzy.

Disorientated.

Not just her head, but every cell in her body seemed to be spinning as he hauled himself from the bed and unlike Lydia, with her sheet-covered dash to the bathroom, his body was hers to view.

And that blasted default switch was stuck, because Lydia did the right thing and averted her eyes.

Yet he didn't walk past. Instead Raul walked right over to her and stood in front of her.

She could feel the heat—not just from his naked body but her own—and it felt as if her dress might disintegrate.

He put his fingers on her chin, tilted her head so that she met his eyes, and it killed that he did not kiss her, nor drag her back to his bed. Instead he checked again. 'Are you sure?'

'Of course,' Lydia said, and tried to make light of it. 'I never say no to a free trip.'

It was a joke but it put her in an unflattering light. She was about to correct herself, to say that it hadn't come out as she had meant, but then she saw his slight smile and it spelt approval.

A gold-digger he could handle, Lydia realised.

Her emerging feelings for him—perhaps not.

At every turn her world changed, and she fought for a semblance of control. Fought to convince not just Raul but herself that she could handle this.